COLLINS
CRIME

THE
SEVEN STARS

Anthea Fraser

Collins Crime
An imprint of HarperCollins*Publishers*
77–85 Fulham Palace Road, London W6 8JB

First published in Great Britain
in 1995 by Collins Crime

1 3 5 7 9 10 8 6 4 2

© Anthea Fraser 1995

The Author asserts the moral right to be
identified as the author of this work

A catalogue record for this book is
available from the British Library

ISBN 0 00 232547 0

Set in Meridien and Bodoni

Photoset by Rowland Phototypesetting Ltd
Bury St Edmunds, Suffolk
Printed and bound in Great Britain by
HarperCollinsManufacturing Glasgow

GREEN GROW THE RUSHES-O

I'll sing you one-O!
(Chorus) Green grow the rushes-O!
       What is your one-O?
One is one and all alone and evermore shall be so.

I'll sing you two-O!
(Chorus) Green grow the rushes-O!
       What are your two-O?
Two, two, the lily-white Boys, clothed all in green-O,
(Chorus) One is one and all alone and evermore shall be so.

I'll sing you three-O!
(Chorus) Green grow the rushes-O!
       What are your three-O?
Three, three, the Rivals,
(Chorus) Two, two, the lily-white Boys, clothed all in green-O,
One is one and all alone and evermore shall be so.

Four for the Gospel makers.
Five for the Symbols at your door.
Six for the six proud Walkers.
Seven for the seven Stars in the sky.
Eight for the April Rainers.
Nine for the nine bright Shiners.
Ten for the ten Commandments.
Eleven for the Eleven that went up to Heaven.
Twelve for the twelve Apostles.

1

For the rest of her life, Helen was to wonder whether, if she had turned left instead of right out of the university gates, events would have turned out differently. Had she herself been the catalyst, or was the course already set and her own part in it negligible?

At the time, however, she had no premonition of the far-reaching consequences of her inattention. In the rear-view mirror, Penelope's figure grew smaller, disappearing completely as a bend in the drive hid her from sight. That was it, then. The Christmas respite was over, both children had returned to college, and this evening she and Andrew would have the house to themselves.

Not that Christmas had been plain sailing, with the strain of trying to behave naturally. She'd read there was a sharp increase in family break-ups following the festive season. Too much enforced goodwill, no doubt.

She waited at the gates as an endless stream of cars swooshed past her. She was later than she'd intended and the murky afternoon was thickening into fog, a hazard she'd not anticipated.

A sudden toot jolted her out of her musings. A motorist was flashing his lights, inviting her to emerge, and she started forward quickly, in her haste turning right towards the town, as they'd done at lunch-time. The motorway lay in the opposite direction.

She could imagine what Andrew's comments would have been, Helen thought grimly as she crawled in line over the viaduct into town. It was a stupid mistake, due entirely to lack of attention, but on reflection no real harm was done.

If she turned right again into the High Street, she should be able to work her way back to the main road.

Then, as she took the turn, she saw the sign for Shillingham. Surely it would be quicker, instead of doubling back, to carry on and join the M4 a couple of junctions nearer London.

She inched her way along the High Street, thronged now as home-going shoppers clogged the road or queued patiently at the bus stops. They'd be glad to get home on such a night. Would she? Home to Andrew's moody silences and outbursts of temper? To Pen and Thomas's empty bedrooms, and the depressing task of stripping their beds?

At the far side of town, a more detailed sign informed her that Shillingham was twenty-seven miles away. Farther than she'd expected, Helen thought, hoping the fog would clear.

Instead, with the lights of the town behind her, visibility worsened. Fog drifted in from the fields on either side, smudging the headlamps of approaching cars, and she realized with dismay that far from correcting her error, she had compounded it.

The road was winding in a leisurely fashion through the countryside, adding miles to the already lengthy drive ahead of her. She should have turned back when she had the chance. If she could find a suitable place, she would do so now.

But no suitable place presented itself and the oncoming traffic was continuous, an unending succession of lights that half blinded her. Behind her temples the first, ominous hints of a headache stirred, a reminder that she was both physically and emotionally exhausted. The prospect of struggling through foggy country lanes to the motorway, only to face a further long drive, was suddenly insupportable.

She should have booked a room for the night, rather than attempt the double journey – plus helping Pen to settle in – in one day.

Another signpost was looming and she narrowed tired eyes to read it. *Marlton 5, Shillingham 18.* A wave of relief washed over her; there'd be somewhere in Marlton where she could spend the night.

In fact, she'd covered only two of those miles when an outline materialized ahead, a building with lights in its windows and an illuminated sign on which, as she drew nearer, she made out the welcome words: *The Seven Stars Guesthouse. Bed and Breakfast.*

Sending up a little prayer of gratitude, Helen turned off the road and, following the car-park sign, drove down the side of the house to where the narrow lane opened up into a large, gravelled space in front of a huddle of outbuildings. A couple of cars were parked at the far end and she drew in beside them.

Switching off her lights, she picked up her handbag and was about to leave the car when a noise from the house made her pause. A door had been flung open and a figure came running out, skirted what looked like a conservatory, and disappeared round the corner she had just negotiated.

A man's voice shouted urgently, 'Molly! Come back! Molly!' and was followed almost immediately by the man himself in hot pursuit. At the corner of the house, however, he hesitated. Then, perhaps because the girl was already out of sight, he turned back towards the house and, without glancing at the darkened cars, went in and slammed the door.

Helen got out and looked about her, shivering in the dank evening. The house was long and sprawling, with a steep gable at each end and the octagonal sun-room or conservatory halfway along. She glanced at the small door through which the figures had emerged. Lights shone behind its glass panes, but she decided against approaching it. Better to use the conventional front entrance.

Diffused light from the house guided her to the corner, from where she could see the blurred aura of a streetlamp on the main road. Picking her way over the uneven ground, she walked back up the lane to the front of the house.

It was an attractive-looking building in the local stone with the same steep gables as at the rear, and these were repeated in miniature above single-storey wings that protruded on either side. Helen walked between them to the arched front door and rang the bell.

Several minutes passed, and she was about to ring again

when the door opened and a tall, red-haired woman of about her own age stood looking at her. Helen said, 'Could I possibly have a room for the night? The fog's thickening and I don't fancy the drive home. You are open, aren't you?'

The woman smiled. 'To benighted travellers, always. Come in.'

Helen stepped into the welcoming warmth and gave an exclamation of pleasure.

The hall was large and inviting. Old beams crisscrossed the ceiling, a huge fire blazed in an open hearth, and in the far corner a couple of men stood drinking at a small bar. They turned curiously to glance at her.

Helen followed her hostess to a small office on the right of the hall. 'I've no luggage, I'm afraid. I wasn't intending to be away overnight.'

'I'm sure we can rustle up something. I'm one of the proprietors, Stella Cain; my sister and I run this place, helped sporadically by our husbands.'

'Helen Campbell.'

Mrs Cain lifted a large registrations book on to the desk, opened it at the current page and turned it to face Helen. 'If you'd like to fill in your name, address and car number, I'll sort some things out for you.' She bent to open a cupboard. 'I keep a stock of toothbrushes, razors and so on; you'd be surprised how often people forget to bring them.'

'Are you open all year?' Helen asked, looking up from the register.

'Not officially, but at the moment we have two residents, whom you saw just now. Mr Pike works in Steeple Bayliss and stays with us Mondays to Thursdays, and Mr Saxton is living here while his house is being converted. Which takes care of our single rooms, but we have a twin and a double free. Actually, you're better off in the twin; it has a proper bathroom *en suite*, while the singles have only shower rooms.'

'A long, hot bath would be bliss,' Helen admitted.

'Fine. And I presume you'll want an evening meal?'

'You do provide it, then?' The sign had said bed and breakfast and she'd been wondering if she could beg a sandwich.

'Normally, only if it's ordered at breakfast, but one more won't make any difference. We eat at seven.'

An hour and a half to relax, Helen thought gratefully. 'Is there a pay phone? I must let my husband know where I am.'

'Yes, it's under the stairs.' Mrs Cain handed her a plastic-wrapped toothbrush and a carton of toothpaste. 'I've a comb if you need it.'

'No thanks, I have one in my bag, and some basic make-up. I'll manage.'

They crossed the hall, from which the men had now disappeared, and started up the shallow staircase. 'How old is the house?' Helen asked.

'Late seventeenth century. It was a coaching inn for many years, then evolved into a pub.'

Helen glanced back at the gracious hall. 'It certainly doesn't look like one now!'

'No, we've restored the original layout. It wasn't too difficult; a ramshackle division had been put in to separate the public bar and saloon, with the bar itself in the middle. We just pulled the lot out and put a small bar-unit discreetly in the corner, as you saw.'

They had reached the top of the stairs. The landing had a decided slope, and the thick blue carpet failed to muffle the creaking boards beneath it. There was a curtained window at each end, beneath which stood small rosewood tables bearing identical arrangements of dried flowers. Mrs Cain turned to the left and, walking the length of the corridor, opened the door at the far end.

'This is at the back of the house,' she said, drawing the curtains. 'It'll be nice and quiet for you. Let me know if there's anything else you need.'

Left alone, Helen looked interestedly about her. The room was charming, its cream walls adorned with old prints, its curtains and matching bedspreads spattered with poppies on a cream background. The plain red carpet was the same luxurious thickness as that on the landing, the furniture attractive in pale wood. A kettle and other tea-making equipment stood invitingly on a shelf.

She pulled the curtain aside and looked out of the window. Beneath her, indistinct in the foggy darkness, lay the gravel courtyard and the blurred humps of the cars. The door through which the girl had run must be directly below her. Idly, Helen wondered what had prompted her flight.

She let the curtain fall and stood uncertainly for a moment. It felt strange having no luggage to unpack, nothing to make the room more personal. Still, a bath would restore her.

She went to the bathroom and turned on the taps, grateful to find a towelling robe on the back of the door. After her bath, she'd wrap herself in it and lie down for a while. Andrew wasn't expecting her for an hour or more yet; time enough to phone him when she went down for dinner. Undressing quickly, she stepped into the bath and sank under the steaming water.

When, shortly before seven, Helen came downstairs, the hall was deserted. Bracing herself, she turned into the short passage which housed the pay phone and her heart began its familiar pounding as she dialled her home number.

'Yes?' Andrew's voice, typically curt and impatient.

'It's me,' she said. 'I'm afraid I shan't be able to get home this evening. It's foggy up here, so I'm staying overnight.'

'Oh, really, Helen! Couldn't you have left earlier?'

'I'm sorry, I didn't realize the time. There's some cold chicken in the fridge, and—'

'When *will* you be home?' he interrupted, as though she were being deliberately difficult.

'About lunch-time, I should think.' She paused. 'Is it foggy there?'

'No, clear as a bell.'

It would be. 'Well, I'll see you tomorrow then.' She paused and when he made no comment, added, 'Goodbye.'

'Goodbye,' he said, and put down the phone. Slowly Helen did the same, waiting for her heartbeat to return to normal. She emerged from the passage and paused, wondering where to go. Suddenly, a voice spoke near at hand, making her jump. It came from behind a half-open door just beside her, in apparent reply to some comment.

'Well, dammit, I thought she'd gone. God knows how much she heard.'

Hastily, in case she too should be thought to be eavesdropping, Helen walked over to the fireplace, her mind returning to her problems.

Something would have to be done, she thought wearily, gazing into the heart of the flames; they couldn't go on like this. Despite her valiant efforts over Christmas, the children had not been deceived. Several times, for no reason, Penelope had caught and squeezed her hand, and once Thomas said diffidently, 'Is everything all right, Mum?'

She reminded herself that they weren't really children any more; perhaps she should be more frank with them. But that would be disloyal to Andrew. She must speak to him first, and her heart quailed at the prospect.

There was a newspaper lying on the chair and, picking it up, Helen seated herself by the fire and began to leaf through it. It was local – the *Broadshire Evening News* – and, like most local papers, carried pages of advertisements. One, prominently displayed in a box, caught her eye.

Melbray Court, Steeple Bayliss.

Registrations are now being accepted
for the following courses:
Art Appreciation – w/e 21st–23rd January
Introducing Antiques – (2 weeks) – 24th January–
6th February
Medieval English – w/e 11th–13th February.

The list continued, but Helen's eyes returned to the two-week course. Until recently, she'd worked part time in an antique shop, becoming increasingly aware of the gaps in her knowledge. It would be fascinating to attempt to fill in some of them.

On impulse, she fished her diary out of her handbag and jotted down the phone number. Then, since nobody had yet appeared, she continued flicking through the paper, pausing again at a horoscope column. A blurred photograph of the forecaster, aptly named Stargazer, graced the top corner.

Mocking herself, Helen read her own sign, noting with wry amusement a warning against rash decisions. When had she ever been rash? Over-caution was her failing.

A separate, boxed entry gave the forecast for 'Tomorrow's Birthday' and since the twelfth of January had been her father's anniversary, she glanced at that, too. *Someone is waiting to hear from you*, it ended. They'd have a long wait, she thought, and in a wave of sadness felt tears come to her eyes. If only he'd been here, she could have talked things over with him as she had so many times.

'Ah, Mrs Campbell!'

Helen started and looked up, blinking back her tears. A man in his late forties, casually smart in blazer and cords, was coming towards her with his hand outstretched.

'Gordon Cain. My wife told me you'd arrived. Can I get you a drink?'

Helen smiled and took his hand, declining the drink. He was of medium height, slightly overweight, and had dark hair and rather high colouring.

'I hear you were caught in the fog. Have you come far?'

'No, only from Steeple Bayliss. I brought my daughter back to university and was late starting home again. But we live in Hampshire, and it seemed too far to go in these conditions.'

He looked surprised. 'You don't use the motorway?'

She smiled ruefully. 'Normally, yes, but I took a wrong turning and decided to join it at Shillingham. But it was farther away than I thought and the fog was getting worse, and then I saw your sign. It just about saved my sanity.'

'I'm glad; you made a wise decision. Much safer to relax here, have a meal and a good night's sleep, and start off again in the morning.'

'Your wife said this used to be a coaching inn?'

'That's right; then it was a pub for donkey's years. Now we've reverted to the original concept – bed and board for the wayfarer, even if we no longer supply a change of horses! The old sign's behind the bar – come and look.'

Helen followed him over and, leaning on the polished surface, studied the ancient, faded board hanging in pride of place on the wall behind. Above spidery letters spelling out its name was a stylized drawing of the constellation of Ursa Major.

Cain said, 'I must confess that although we fell for the place, it was the name that clinched it for me. I've always been interested in astrology. In fact, my wife's been known to say the only reason I married her is because her name's Stella!'

Helen smiled. 'It's a wonder it wasn't called the Plough, like so many pubs.'

'There was certainly plenty of choice – the Plough, as you say, the Great Bear, King Charles's Wain, the Waggon – they're all names for the same constellation. We had some American visitors last summer, and they referred to it as the Big Dipper, which sounds more like a fairground to me.'

Helen had started to speak when a loud banging sounded on the front door, together with the simultaneous and continuous ringing of the bell.

'What the devil –?'

Gordon Cain went hurrying to answer it as his wife and another woman came quickly into the hall, exclaiming at the commotion. From where she stood, Helen couldn't see the door but she caught the urgent exchange of voices and a moment later Cain came quickly back, followed by a pale and breathless young man.

Mrs Cain started forward. 'Gordon, whatever –?'

'There's been an accident along the road,' he answered tersely, striding into the office. 'I'm ringing for an ambulance.'

The young man hovered between the office door and the powerful magnet of the fire. He had started to shiver, doubtless from shock as much as the cold outside.

'She was lying at the side of the road,' he said jerkily. 'My girlfriend spotted her; she was peering out of the window to see how near the edge we were – it's really thick out there. She thought it was a heap of clothes at first, but we decided to stop and make sure. Thank God we did.'

'Which way were you going?' Stella Cain asked.

15

'Towards Marlton, but since we'd only just passed you, it seemed quickest to come back here to phone.'

Stella glanced towards the door. 'Wouldn't your friend like to come in?'

'She stayed with the girl. We didn't dare move her so we rigged up a torch as a warning light.'

'Is she badly hurt?' Helen asked.

He shrugged. 'She's unconscious; it's hard to tell.'

Gordon Cain emerged from the office. 'They're on their way.'

'Cheers. I'd better get back to Lesley. I didn't like leaving her.'

'Shall I come with you?' Cain offered.

'Thanks, but it's OK. There's really nothing you can do, and the ambulance shouldn't be long.' With a nod that included them all, he turned and hurried back outside.

Detective Chief Inspector Webb swore under his breath. It was getting thicker than ever, dammit. At this rate he'd be late for his meeting with the Ledbetters.

It had seemed a good idea at the time; the Gallery of Modern Art at SB was showing some Russian paintings, and, knowing his interest, Chris had suggested Webb met him and his wife there and went back with them for supper afterwards. Since he'd nothing urgent at the moment, he'd accepted and left the station at six, which in all conscience should have allowed comfortable time for the journey. But the mist which had been barely noticeable in Shillingham had progressively thickened, and after Marlton became almost impenetrable. What's more, he thought gloomily, there was the return journey to bear in mind.

It was as he cautiously rounded a bend that he noticed a faint light on the far side of the road. He slowed down still further, peering through the opaque darkness in an attempt to identify it. Then a figure took shape behind the light, which he recognized as a torch. He pulled up and wound down the window.

'Are you in trouble?' he called.

'Yes, someone's been knocked down.' It was a young

16

female voice, trembling with tension. 'My boyfriend's gone to phone for an ambulance.'

Webb inched his car up on to the verge and got out. 'Did you see what happened?'

'No. We were creeping along in the fog and I was watching the nearside verge and – and saw her lying there.'

Webb peered down at the prostrate form on the ground, and his heart sank. He'd seen enough dead bodies to recognize at once that this was another. Nevertheless, he bent to feel the carotid artery. No sign of a pulse. He looked up at the slim figure above him.

'I'm afraid an ambulance will be no use to her,' he said gently.

'You mean she's dead? But I've been talking to her! I thought it might somehow get through. Oh, God!' She sounded on the brink of tears.

Webb straightened. 'I'll get on to the police,' he said. 'I'm Chief Inspector Webb. And you're –?'

'Lesley Brown, and my boyfriend's Martin Skinner.' She looked up at him, her mouth trembling. 'Is there anything we should have done? The kiss of life –?'

'I'm sure there wasn't,' he assured her. 'She probably died instantly. It was madness, walking along here in these conditions – she must have known no one could see her.'

He got his mobile phone from the car and called Control at Force HQ. 'And I'd like to request a diversion,' he ended. 'The less traffic we have along here, the better.'

He had just finished speaking when the sound of a slowly approaching car reached them and a moment later twin headlights bloomed through the fog. Lesley Brown flashed her torch, the car drew to a halt and the driver climbed out. She ran towards him, flinging herself into his arms.

'Martin, there's a policeman here, and he says she's dead!'

Webb moved forward. 'You got through to the ambulance service, sir?'

Skinner nodded, swallowing nervously. 'You are sure? That she's dead?'

'I'm afraid so.'

17

'But – surely whoever it was must have known they'd hit her?'

'Almost definitely.'

'And they just left her lying there? It's unbelievable! If they'd acted straight away, they might have saved her.' He started to move towards the body, but Webb gently stopped him.

'We need to preserve the scene, sir; there might be traces of the vehicle that hit her.'

'Yes, yes, of course.'

'I suggest you and the young lady wait in your car.'

They nodded and, with barely concealed relief, complied while Webb, pulling up his coat collar against the freezing night air, settled down to await reinforcements.

As their visitor hurried away, Cain closed and bolted the door behind him.

'Well!' Stella said with a nervous little laugh, 'after all that, dinner's ready. Mrs Campbell, this is my sister, Kate Warren.'

Helen had gathered so, though there was no overt similarity between the women other than their height. Unlike her sister's red hair, Mrs Warren's was dark, as were her eyes, and she struck Helen as the more reserved of the two.

However, she smiled and nodded pleasantly as they moved across the hall to the dining-room. It was furnished in period, with gleaming dark wood, ladder-back chairs and a grandfather clock whose dial showed the phases of the moon. On the opposite wall, full-length curtains in heavy green velvet hid the windows, and a spotlight had been positioned to lighten their otherwise sombre richness. In the centre of the room, to Helen's surprise, stood one long table laid for seven.

'I hope you don't mind,' Stella Cain said quickly. 'When there are so few of us, we eat together in the evenings.'

As Helen pulled out a chair, the two men she'd seen earlier came in and Stella introduced them. Michael Saxton, who had seated himself opposite Helen, had an interesting if rather severe face, with character lines between his eyebrows and at the corners of his mouth. She imagined he could

18

drive a hard bargain. He looked about fifty, and his plentiful, lightish brown hair was liberally sprinkled with grey.

Terry Pike, who had taken the chair on her right, was taller and thinner, in his early forties at a guess. His hair, dull and dark, was cut jaggedly in a style which struck Helen as just a little too youthful. He had a broad nose set in a long face and a slight north-country accent.

'We were watching Channel 4 News,' Michael Saxton said. 'There's been another of those Stately Home burglaries, though they're not sure when it took place. The owners have just discovered something missing.'

'The servants probably nicked it,' Kate Warren said dismissively. 'You missed our own little drama; didn't you hear all the commotion?'

The two men looked surprised. 'No, what happened?'

As she finished telling them, the door leading to the kitchen opened and Gordon Cain appeared, holding it wide for a tall, grey-haired man who emerged balancing a tray of soup bowls.

'Can you manage, darling?' Kate Warren started to push back her chair.

'Stay where you are – everything's under control.' Helped by his brother-in-law, Warren began to unload the steaming bowls and a plate of hot rolls.

'Just the fare for a night like this. Did anyone hear the forecast?'

'The fog will last all night and clear slowly in the morning,' Terry Pike quoted.

Warren glanced at Helen. 'Mrs Campbell, I presume. I'm Nicholas Warren, this evening's chef.'

'Correction!' his wife interposed. 'He made the soup – it's one of his specialities – but his contribution to the rest of the meal was minimal.'

Helen said diplomatically, 'It smells delicious.'

Nicholas Warren was a good-looking man, with regular features, deep-set grey eyes and a firm mouth, and Helen didn't doubt he was used to getting exactly what he wanted.

An interesting quartet, she reflected, and not at all as one imagined landlords and ladies. But then she'd read an article

19

recently on a new breed of B & B proprietors, who might be anything from retired ambassadors and their wives, who were used to entertaining and enjoyed having guests, to couples whose families had left home and who appreciated the ever-changing company as well as the income it brought.

'Have you been open long?' she asked Stella across the table.

'This is our third year. I wanted something to do when our daughter left home, and Nicholas and Kate had just come back after years abroad and were looking for somewhere to live. So we decided to pool our resources and buy this place. Generally speaking, the men deal with the business side and Kate and I see to the day-to-day running of it. It works very well.'

Helen was gratified that her assessment of the situation had been so accurate. The meal was excellent, the soup being followed by a rich casserole, an interesting selection of cheeses and a frothy lemon soufflé. Conversation was relaxed and general, and she noted that the two 'residents' were on first-name terms with their hosts, making their careful use of her own surname sound stilted. Still, in this group she was merely the ship that passed in the night.

Exhaustion had claimed her by the time coffee was served, and shortly afterwards she went up to her room. Before getting into bed, she again looked out of the window, hoping that the fog might have thinned. But it was wrapped tightly round the building, its thick dampness pressing against the windowpanes and obscuring even the courtyard below.

Shivering, Helen slipped off the towelling robe and, of necessity, slipped naked between the sheets.

2

During the last couple of hours the familiar procedure had gradually established itself. The ambulance crew were the first to arrive, and, finding their services not required, went away again. Then two uniformed police constables from Marlton appeared, one of whom startled Webb by recognizing the victim.

'Why, that's Jack Flint's girl!' he'd exclaimed, shock ringing in his voice. 'They live just across from us!' Which identification remained their only piece of luck on this bleak, bone-freezing night. Not that the luck extended to the PC, who would later have to inform his neighbours of the tragedy.

The next to arrive were DI Ledbetter and DS Hopkins from Steeple Bayliss. 'Not quite the evening we'd planned, Dave,' Ledbetter commented after Webb had outlined the position. 'Still, we might be able to salvage something out of it when we've got this lot sorted.'

The road had been closed for several hundred yards in both directions and diversion signs set up at Marlton to the east and just short of Steeple Bayliss to the west.

Those attending the scene were directed to park several metres down the road on the opposite side to the accident. Which, Webb reflected glumly, had a touch of the stable door about it, since there was no knowing how much traffic had passed between the time of death and the arrival of the couple who reported it.

Slowly the evening wore on. The local police surgeon attended, certified death and departed again as swiftly as decency allowed. Webb didn't blame him. Then, with the arrival of the SOCOs and the Coroner's Officer, the tempo of the investigation at last accelerated. Arc lights were rigged up, a tent was erected to protect the scene, and the exhaustive videoing and photographing began.

Finally, just as the SOCOs were finishing, the pathologist appeared, his diminutive body emerging from the foggy darkness muffled in scarves and with his hat pulled well down on his head.

Ledbetter and Webb, skirting the scene, moved to join him.

Stapleton peered irritably into their faces. 'That you, Chief Inspector? Bit off course, aren't you?'

'Believe it or not, Doctor, it's my evening off.'

The little man grunted dismissively and turned his attention to the body, his pale eyes behind their rimless glasses missing no detail of the pathetic huddle on the ground. It was several minutes before he straightened again, fastidiously brushing traces of dirt from his trousers.

'Well, apart from confirming death there's little I can do here. We'll have to wait till we get her to the mortuary.'

'Any chance she was dead before she was hit?' Ledbetter asked. 'Thrown out of a car, then run over to make it look accidental?'

'Judging by the amount of blood, that seems unlikely. Do I take it no one witnessed the accident?'

'No one's come forward. A young couple found her lying there. They've been taken to Marlton for interviewing, but I doubt if they can tell us more than they already have.' Ledbetter turned to Webb. 'Provided, that is, we take their word for what happened. I suppose there's an outside chance it was their car that hit her?'

Webb shrugged. 'We'll have to wait for the examination, but they seem genuine enough. How does the timing fit? I got here about seven, some fifteen minutes after they claim to have found her. How long do you reckon she's been dead, Doctor?'

Stapleton smiled thinly. 'The eternal question. At a rough guess, about three hours. No rigor mortis yet, though admittedly it would be delayed in this temperature.'

Ledbetter angled his wrist so that the light shone on his watch. 'It's now twenty-one-fifteen, which puts the probable time of death at around eighteen hundred, i.e. an hour or so before she was found. That would put the young folk in the clear.'

'It could be an hour either way,' Stapleton said repressively. 'I'll be able to tell you more after a thorough examination. In the meantime, gentlemen, I'll leave you to your deliberations.' And he disappeared into the enfolding fog.

Ledbetter turned to the men awaiting instructions. 'Right, you can bag her up and remove her now. Who's accompanying her to the mortuary?'

Webb intervened. 'As you know, Chris, I found the body, but I've deputed PC Rendle to escort it from the scene.' He indicated one of the Marlton men. The other had been dispatched some time ago to break the news to the relatives.

Ledbetter nodded and supervised the grim business of bagging the body and carrying it to the waiting hearse, after which he detailed the men who would remain overnight to guard the scene. Finally he turned back to Webb.

'OK, that's about it, Dave; nothing more to be done till first light. Too bad about the exhibition, but I bet you're ready for that hot meal. I'll let Janet know we're on our way.'

Webb hesitated. 'Look, Chris, perhaps I should take a rain check. God knows how long it'll take me to get home as it is. I'll have to work my way round the lanes, which will be tricky in this weather.'

'Nonsense, you're spending the night with us. No problem at all,' he continued over Webb's perfunctory protest. 'Wouldn't hear of you setting off again in this. Anyway, Janet's cooking a special meal and I've a wine I'd like you to try; we brought it back from France last summer and have been saving it for a suitable occasion. It's been warming up nicely all day. Which,' he added, clapping frozen hands together, 'is more than I have! This your car? See you back at the house, then.'

Getting into the relative warmth of his car, Webb allowed

himself a sigh of relief. Some pleasant company and a good meal would do a lot to dispel the depression and discomfort of the last few hours, specially since he'd be spared the worry of the drive home. Something would after all be salvaged from his disastrous 'free evening'.

Feeling more cheerful by the minute, he turned the ignition key and, keeping well in to the verge, moved off slowly in the direction of Steeple Bayliss.

When Helen woke the next morning, the pale patch that was the window was in the wrong position, and, disorientated, it took her a moment or two to realize where she was. Then she remembered: the fog, and the Seven Stars rising, Brigadoon-like, out of it. Remembered, too, the dramatic arrival of the young man and his story, and hoped the accident victim was recovering from her ordeal.

She switched on the bedside light and looked at her watch. It was seven-thirty. Sitting up, she reached for the robe, shrugged into it, and, padding to the window, lifted the curtain. It was barely light, but the fog seemed to be lifting. By the time she was ready to leave, it should be almost clear.

Breakfast, she discovered half an hour later, was served in the garden room she had seen from the courtyard. Terry Pike, whom she met in the hall, directed her to it through the television lounge.

Despite being of glass on three sides, the room was warm and welcoming, since radiators encircled it beneath the windows. The effect was pleasantly spring-like, with the sandy-coloured tiled floor, round, glass-topped tables and cream lattice-back chairs with green cushions.

Michael Saxton, reading his newspaper at one of the tables, looked up briefly to bid her good morning.

In the centre of the room was a table bearing a selection of fruit, yoghurts, cereals and juices. Helen poured a glass of orange juice and seated herself in what would have been the bay window, had the rest of the walls had not also been of glass.

Stella Cain appeared, teapot in one hand, coffeepot in the

other. 'Good morning, Mrs Campbell. Would you like a full English breakfast or the continental?'

Helen opted for the continental, and indicated the coffee-pot. As Mrs Cain moved away, she looked interestedly out of the window for her first daylight view of her surroundings.

To her left was a patio area surrounded by a two-foot stone wall and covered by a pergola, which in summer would no doubt be entwined with flowers. Alongside it was the door through which the man and girl had come running last night.

Immediately opposite, across the gravelled courtyard, lay the group of outbuildings. They were of the same stone as the house, with small-paned windows and steeply pitched tile roof – probably the original mews, Helen thought, coachmen's quarters above, stables below, but they'd been extensively renovated. Perhaps that was where her hosts slept; there weren't enough doors along the landing to accommodate them, nor had she noticed a staircase to an upper floor.

The figure of Terry Pike crossed her line of vision, and she watched as he unlocked the car next to her own and drove out of the area.

Her attention was brought back to the table by the arrival of hot croissants. 'And I thought you might like a paper,' Stella said, laying a copy of the *Daily Telegraph* beside her plate.

Helen thanked her and glanced at the front page. The main story was the latest in what the press had dubbed the 'Stately Home Burglaries', though Andrew, who worked for a firm of loss adjusters, referred to them more accurately as country houses, since not all of them warranted the grander title.

The robberies had been taking place at irregular intervals for a couple of years now and were spread over a wide area. Every few months a manor house somewhere in the country was robbed, and in each case only one specific item was taken: a priceless miniature, a ruby necklace, a set of vinaigrettes.

Such exploits had already cost the insurance companies over a million pounds, but an intriguing sidelight was that occasionally the stolen object, though unusual or attractive, was worth less than a hundred pounds and of only sentimental value. But none of the items had been recovered, nor did the police seem any nearer to identifying the culprits.

The latest theft was at Plaistead Manor in Gloucestershire, but as the loss had only just been noticed and there was no sign of a break-in, the police wouldn't confirm it was the same operator. The stolen object was a signed miniature of Queen Victoria in a silver frame studded with tiny diamonds. It had been presented to a previous Lady Plaistead, a favourite lady-in-waiting.

Intent on the story, Helen had not heard Terry Pike return, and jumped as his voice said from the doorway, 'The blasted road's closed. I thought you'd like to know.'

Michael Saxton exclaimed with annoyance. 'Closed where?'

'A few hundred yards along, towards Marlton. Presumably traffic between there and SB has been diverted. God knows how far I'll have to backtrack before I can weave round again, and I've an appointment at nine-thirty.'

'Thanks for letting us know.'

Helen said anxiously, 'Does that mean I can't get through to Shillingham? I was going to join the M4 there.'

'You'll be able to loop round, no doubt,' Saxton replied, as the other man hurried out. 'Though your best bet, since you'll have to double back towards Steeple Bayliss anyway, would be to join it there.'

As, Helen reflected ruefully, she should have done in the first place.

Twenty minutes later she had paid her modest bill and was on her way. The fog still lingered in the distance and moisture drenched the hedgerows and hung from the branches of trees, but at least she could see where she was going.

She came to the diversion sign a few miles short of Steeple Bayliss and, having driven past, stopped to look back at it. It directed traffic down a narrow country lane surprisingly signposted: *Melbray Court 2, M4 16.* So she needn't go into Steeple Bayliss after all. If she'd spotted that signpost last night, she reflected, she would doubtless have turned off there.

It seemed an unlikely route to the motorway, this narrow, high-hedged lane; probably it was used mainly by local people wanting to bypass Steeple Bayliss. After a couple of miles a right-hand fork led to Melbray Court. Helen frowned, wondering why the name seemed familiar, then remembered the advertisement she'd cut out. It was a wonder anyone found the place, she thought.

After a few miles she emerged from the tunnel-like lane to join what she recognized as the main road from Steeple Bayliss to the motorway, and, turning thankfully on to it, she settled down for the long drive home.

Having checked that there was nothing urgent in Shillingham to claim his attention, Webb decided to stay on in SB for the postmortem, scheduled for ten o'clock that morning. As he enjoyed a leisurely breakfast with his hosts, he was struck again by their seeming mismatch.

It was frequently remarked – though never in his hearing – that Chris Ledbetter looked more like a male model than a policeman, with his thick blond hair and gentian-blue eyes; whereas Janet, his wife, was a mousey-haired woman with a small, pinched face and a shy smile. Nevertheless, theirs was an extremely happy union, which, Webb reflected, was a bonus in their line of business.

'How's Sergeant Jackson's family?' Janet asked, as she topped up his teacup. 'The twins must be toddlers now; I remember you were here the day they were born.'

'So I was.' Webb thought back to that fraught evening nearly three years ago, when, coincidentally, he had just found another dead girl. 'They're all thriving, and though he tries to hide it, Ken's as proud as Punch of the lot of them.'

Janet Ledbetter looked at him thoughtfully. She had often wondered if Dave regretted having no family, but it was hardly a question she could ask. His marriage had ended in divorce nearly nine years ago, and though she gathered from Chris there was some woman in his life, no one seemed to know who she was. Which, considering police-station gossip, said a great deal for his discretion.

'Well' – Chris looked up at the kitchen clock – 'we'd better be making tracks. Let's hope that good breakfast stays down!'

The mortuary at Steeple Bayliss was attached to the West Broadshire Hospital in Gloucester Road. But no matter what the location, the atmosphere – and especially the unmistakable smell – was always the same and, as always, filled Webb with a queasy sense of depression.

The postmortem room, also as usual, was fairly crowded. Webb nodded to the Coroner's Officer and to PC Rendle, who was providing continuity of evidence. SOCOs were arranging their cameras to record the procedure and the video was already in position.

On the slab in the centre of the room lay the cause of all this activity, her long hair tousled, her spiky mascaraed lashes lying incongruously on pale cheeks. She looked so fragile, Webb thought, so vulnerable – as, indeed, she had proved to be.

Then Stapleton pressed the pedal to start the tape recorder and spoke into the microphone suspended over his head. The operation was about to begin.

At the end of an hour and a half, the young body had given up all the information of which it was capable. Tread marks had patterned the skin through the clothing, but bruising would take another thirty-six hours to develop fully and the body would be re-examined then. Basically, though, and in layman's terms, she had been crushed to death, which was no surprise. Nor were there any marks consistent with prior attack; she appeared to have been alive when the car hit her.

'Just one point, Doctor,' Chris Ledbetter said, as Stapleton turned off the tape recorder. 'The body, as you know, was found on the left-hand verge; that is, she had her back to oncoming traffic. Yet she was lying on her back and the principal injuries appear to be to her chest and abdomen.'

'I had noted that, Inspector,' Stapleton said drily. 'All I can assume is that at the last minute she heard the car coming

28

and spun round, either in a futile attempt to ward it off, or possibly to hitch a lift.'

Which, Webb acknowledged as he and Ledbetter walked out of the building, seemed reasonable enough.

'Let me know how you get on,' he said as they reached his car. 'I hope you catch the bastard.'

'Amen to that. Sorry last night wasn't quite what we planned. Another time, perhaps.'

'It was a first-class meal and the wine was memorable. My thanks again to you both.'

And, glad to have the postmortem behind him, he drove out of the hospital gateway and turned in the direction of Shillingham.

The nearer Helen came to reaching home, the more depressed she grew. The house would seem empty without the children and, more importantly, there would be no buffer between herself and Andrew.

They used to be happy, she thought sadly. When had things started to go wrong? Or had there always been that underlying uncertainty, that awareness of having to think before she spoke? Certainly he'd always had a temper, but she'd had the knack of dealing with him then, of defusing his outbursts before they got out of hand. Perhaps it was she who'd changed rather than he.

As long as the children were at home, she'd been able to conceal her worries, even from herself. If Andrew was in a mood, or, as increasingly happened, spent the evening at the golf club, at least she had them for company. Then Thomas went away to medical school and, last October, Penelope started at Broadshire University. And at the end of the same month, by way of a final straw, Helen lost her job.

Before her marriage, and, in fact, up to her first pregnancy, she had worked at one of the big London auction houses, enjoying the bustle, the excitement over successful sales, the handling of beautiful things. In fact, it was there she'd met Andrew, who at the time was working as a valuer.

She had therefore been delighted, once both children were at school, to find a part-time job in the local antique shop.

It wasn't well paid, but that didn't worry her. It gave her an interest outside the home, and, though a poor reflection of her pre-marriage career, she enjoyed the work.

Until last year, when the recession finally caught up with Past Times, and Joan Barrett, the owner, was forced to close down. Helen had been almost as upset as she was; for Joan's sake, but also because the days ahead were now frighteningly blank.

Nor had Andrew been sympathetic. 'A lot of people would be glad to have time to themselves,' he'd said. 'I for one.'

'No, you wouldn't!' Helen contradicted him.

'Well, you can fill your days easily enough. Go out for coffee, take up golf, do good works. Join a club!' he'd added sardonically, repeating the standard advice to those at a loose end.

But the thought of an endless round of coffee mornings filled Helen with panic, and she had no interest in golf. Although she volunteered to help with the library service and to deliver Meals on Wheels, long hours still remained unfilled.

It wasn't easy for a forty-something woman to find work, she reflected, as she approached the small market town where she lived. Perhaps she should train for something specific, take an Open University course. But on what?

As she reached the High Street the church clock was chiming midday and the Wednesday market was in full swing. Bridget, her next-door neighbour, was talking to old Mrs Cummings, and further along Mary Stanton was judiciously feeling avocados at one of the stalls. They seemed contented enough with their golf and their bridge and their daily shopping trips. Was there something the matter with her, that she needed more?

She turned off Market Street, drove down several pleasant roads, and was finally home. With a sigh she collected her handbag and let herself into the house. The first thing she'd do was strip the children's beds and get the sheets into the machine.

She dropped her handbag on the hall table and went up to her daughter's room. The bed was still rumpled, there was a handkerchief on the floor and a paperback face-down on a chair.

Suppressing a renewed wave of misery, Helen seized the bottom sheet, pulling it free, and as she did so, caught an image of herself in the long wardrobe mirror. She let the sheet fall and moved slowly towards her reflection, assessing, taking stock.

Not too bad, considering. She lent closer to the glass, her eyes moving critically from one feature to the next. There were lines round eyes and mouth that hadn't been there a few years ago, but the eyes themselves were still clear and returned her gaze candidly. The hair which hung loose round her face was still a shining mid-brown, though one or two silver threads were visible, particularly at the temples. She turned sideways on, patting her stomach. Again, not bad, though a little more exercise mightn't go amiss. But she wasn't over the hill yet; all she asked was the chance to prove it.

Having geared herself to meet Andrew that evening, Helen found her apprehension was unfounded. 'Welcome home!' he greeted her, planting a kiss on her cheek. 'Fog clear up all right?'

'Yes, by this morning,' she answered, a little disconcerted. 'I'm sorry about not getting back. Did you have a reasonable meal?'

'I made do with cornflakes and toast,' he replied, dumping his briefcase on a chair.

'Oh, Andrew!' She'd thought the chicken looked much as she left it. Was this, she wondered, an attempt to make her feel guilty, or had he simply eaten what he'd fancied? If she ever left him – the thought came unexpectedly into her head – was that what he'd dine on every night?

To banish the idea, she said quickly, 'I see there's been another country house job.'

'Looks like it, though with no sign of break-in we can't be sure. The family did a lot of entertaining over the Christmas period, and it's quite possible one of the guests pocketed it. But it's made us look again at some of the other robberies that have made the headlines. *If* the same gang did Plaistead Manor, they could be responsible for others we hadn't connected with them.'

'Which in particular?'

'Well, there was the night two bedrooms at the Savoy were broken into. Again, money and other valuables were ignored and only particular items stolen. Then there was that American woman, who "lost" her sapphire and diamond clip between Claridge's and the opera. She remembers someone brushing against her as she got out of the cab, but thought nothing of it at the time. Both cases are worth another look.'

He walked through to the dining-room and she heard him pouring drinks. 'What's for dinner?' he called.

'Would you believe curried chicken?'

'Fine. I'll open a bottle of wine to celebrate your return.'

Helen could think of no reply. He came back and handed her a glass of gin and tonic.

'Here's to the restoration of peace!' he said. 'Or don't you want to drink to that?'

She looked at him quickly and he added, more gently than he'd spoken to her in months, 'I know you miss them, love, but it's all part of life's rich pattern. We raise the chicks and in due time they have to stretch their wings. But it'll soon be Easter and they'll return to the coop.'

She said unsteadily, 'Not a very happy metaphor, when it's chicken for dinner!'

He laughed. 'Well, at least you've still got the old cock!' And he bent and kissed her mouth.

She continued with her cooking in a whirl of mixed emotions. Had the estrangement been all in her mind? Had she overreacted? Or was it just that he was in a good mood and prepared to be sociable? Whatever the reason, she could only be thankful for it.

3

Hannah said, 'So you never got to the exhibition?'

Webb shook his head. 'Pity, really; it would have been worth seeing.'

'Won't you have the chance to go back?'

'I doubt it, it's only on this week. Never mind, there'll be others.'

He leaned back comfortably in Hannah's apple-green chair and swirled the whisky in his glass. Briefly he thought back to the previous evening, and the warm domesticity of the Ledbetters' home. This was a fair replica, though only on the surface – which, he reminded himself, was what they both wanted. Of independent character and fulfilled by their own careers, neither was willing to submit to the bonds of marriage. At least, that was the theory.

In any event, the arrangement had worked admirably for some years now, with only the occasional hiccup. Sometimes, though they lived on different floors in the same building, they didn't meet for weeks, keeping in touch with an occasional phone-call. Sometimes they met as friends, discussing each other's work and topics of the moment. And sometimes – quite often, thankfully, he thought with an inward grin – they spent the night together, conscious of a closeness and fulfilment deeper than either had found elsewhere.

He looked fondly across at Hannah as she gazed into the fire, at the clear brow, the widely spaced grey eyes and the honey-coloured hair that framed her face. He was damned lucky, and when things got him down he needed to remind himself of that.

'Will they find whoever hit the girl?' she asked suddenly, breaking into his thoughts.

Webb shrugged. 'They'll have been scouring the area today and should have come up with something. It's unlikely there were any witnesses, though; it was a deserted stretch of road, quite apart from the fog.' He drained his glass. 'Anyway, not my pigeon, thank God.

'What's so damned stupid,' he added, as Hannah refilled his glass, 'is that if whoever it was had reported it, he might have been in the clear. She was walking on the wrong side and visibility was minimal – he probably didn't see her till he was on top of her. It's the fact that he didn't stop that's so damning.'

'Perhaps he did stop, saw she was dead, and panicked.'

'Possibly. Anyway, enough of that. What have you been doing with yourself? New term started well?'

The head of Ashbourne School for Girls was on a year's sabbatical, leaving Hannah, as her deputy, in temporary charge.

'Heaven knows, it can only be better than the last,' she answered soberly.

There was no denying the previous term had been a baptism of fire. Webb's mouth quirked ruefully as he reflected on the appropriateness of the phrase: a New Age religious cult had set up in town and members of Hannah's school became involved with it, with devastating consequences.

'All I ask,' she continued, 'is that we have a quiet, uneventful few months and a chance to get our breath back. We need to rebuild confidence, both in the school and in ourselves.'

Webb was silent, knowing easy platitudes to be unacceptable. Casting round for something to distract her, he had an inspiration.

'I've a free weekend coming up; how about going off somewhere? London perhaps – take in a concert or a show – or even Paris, if you like?'

Since Hannah's reputation had to be above suspicion they avoided being seen together locally, which for the most part confined them to visiting each other's flats. In any case, his unsocial hours of work meant he could seldom make

34

advance arrangements. Whereas, Webb thought with recurring frustration, Charles bloody Frobisher could – and did – sweep her off to dinners and theatres whenever the mood took him. Or, to be more accurate, whenever Hannah agreed to go with him.

'That sounds wonderful!' she exclaimed now. 'Which weekend is it?'

'The one after next – twenty-second/twenty-third.'

Her face fell. 'Oh, David, I'm so sorry, I can't. We've been invited to the Rudges' party that Saturday.'

Webb's eyes narrowed. 'Who's "we"?'

'The other governors.' She didn't meet his eye. 'You know Sir Clifford's on the board? He throws a party for us every year around this time. It's always very sumptuous.'

'I bet it is,' Webb returned sourly. Frobisher would be there, then. As chairman of the governors, he was probably the bloody guest of honour.

'He was really shaken by that burglary,' Hannah was continuing. 'They took a Georgian wine-taster – worth over fifty thousand, so I heard. It was extremely rare because it was British, and only a few are known to exist.'

'Well, if it's any consolation, the thieves wouldn't get anything like that for it,' Webb commented. 'I suppose we must be thankful the Rudge place is the only country house break-in we've had in Broadshire. So far,' he added grimly.

'No doubt Sir Clifford's television programme made him a likely target. Still, it could have been a lot worse; the Hall's crammed with antiques; if they'd filled their coffers there, they wouldn't have needed to rob anywhere else!'

'But as we've seen, that's not how they work. They know exactly what they're after – usually the pride of the collection – and leave everything else behind.

'Mind you, what really gets me is when they ignore the treasure and take off with something relatively worthless. It's as though they're cocking a snook at us, calmly walking in and taking whatever they fancy.'

He took another drink of whisky. 'One of these days, I keep telling myself, they'll make a mistake, leave a clue of some sort, and then we'll nab them. But they're certainly giving Regional Crime a run for their money.'

'When they *are* caught, what are the chances of getting anything back?'

'Pretty slim, I'd say. Since none of the jewellery has turned up on the international markets, they must have someone on hand to break up and reset it. Considering the quality of the stones they've nicked, that alone would bring them in a fortune. As for the rest, nearly everything they take is small and easily transportable. It's probably whipped straight out to the continent or wherever and passed on almost before it's missed.'

'It must be heartbreaking for the owners,' Hannah said.

'Not as heartbreaking as for the insurance companies! They've paid out millions in the last couple of years.' He glanced at his watch. 'Anyway, my love, I advise you to keep the tiaras in the bank till we've collared this lot!'

She smiled, looking up at him as he got to his feet. 'Going home?'

'Unless I've a better offer.'

'You only have to ask!' she said demurely, and allowed herself to be pulled into his arms.

The truce with Andrew lasted for exactly a week, though during that time Helen was conscious of continually nursing it along, keeping from him things that would annoy him – a request for cash from Thomas, for instance – and avoiding any topic which might lead to controversy. For his part, Andrew spent several evenings at home, complimented her on her appearance more than once, and kept his temper.

But the strain was beginning to show, and although in the event it was she who was at fault, the equilibrium would not have lasted much longer.

The phone-call came at ten-thirty one night. Andrew had gone out to play snooker and Helen, bored by an evening of indifferent television, had gone to bed early and was sound asleep. The strident ringing jerked her awake and she reached fumblingly for the phone.

'Mrs Campbell? This is Ron Goodman. Sorry to call so late. Is your husband there?'

She pushed the hair out of her eyes and looked blearily at the clock. Not the middle of the night, as she'd supposed. 'No, I'm afraid he isn't.'

'I meant to ring earlier but something came up. Could you give him a message? The boss has called a meeting for nine o'clock, so would you ask him to go straight to the office and not to Winchester as we'd arranged?'

'All right.'

'Thanks. Sorry to trouble you,' he said, and rang off. Helen dropped the phone on its cradle, thankfully sliding back into sleep, and the phone-call, like the dreams that followed it, dissolved and faded from her mind.

She didn't give it another thought until Andrew's return the next evening, when it was instantly obvious that something was wrong. He slammed his briefcase on the table and glared at her.

'Was there a phone-call for me last night?'

She stared at him blankly as memory stirred at the back of her mind.

'Well? Was there, or wasn't there?'

'Oh Andrew,' she said, stricken. 'I'm so sorry. It went completely out of my head.'

'It went completely out of your head. Well, that's just fine. So I go shooting off to Winchester as arranged and sit twiddling my thumbs for an hour, and when I ring the office to see what's happened to Ron, I discover I've missed an important meeting.'

She gazed at him aghast. 'I really am terribly sorry. I was asleep – the phone woke me – and this morning I'd completely forgotten about it.'

'And that's the best you can do? God knows, it's not as though you've anything else to think about! If your memory's so abysmal, you should have written it down and left me a note.'

'Look, I've said I'm sorry. Going on about it isn't going to change anything.'

'Well, I've made damn sure it won't happen again. I've

told them at the office always to phone back in future, rather than leave a message which there's no guarantee I'd get.'

She flushed. 'That's not fair. You know I – '

'I felt an absolute idiot, being in the wrong place at the wrong time, and when I finally got to the office, Frank had to go through the whole thing again for my benefit. You can imagine how much that pleased him. All in all, it's been the hell of a day, thanks to you.'

'Well, it's over now,' she said, trying to restore a more equable atmosphere. 'Why don't you pour yourself a drink while I – '

But he had turned on his heel and left the room. Helen drew a deep breath and went on preparing the meal.

It was a miserable evening. Andrew refused to be drawn by her attempts at conversation. He sat in total silence reading the papers, and she realized despairingly that this was just what she had dreaded. Without the children, there was no need to smooth over the cracks in their relationship. Perhaps evenings like this were all they had to look forward to.

She made a last, desperate effort. 'Look, Andrew, snap out of it, for pity's sake. It's not the end of the world. I was at fault and I apologized. What more do you want?'

'It's not as though you've anything else to think about,' he said again.

Her patience snapped. 'No, not a thing!' she flared. 'My mind is a total vacuum. Fortunately I'm programmed to cook your meals, wash your clothes, do the shopping and drive the car, but not to take messages! You'd better trade me in for a newer model!'

He had put down the paper and was staring at her, and she realized it was the first time in twenty-two years that she had lost her temper with him. Until now, that had been his prerogative.

With trembling hands she collected the coffee cups, took them through to the kitchen, and went upstairs without returning to the sitting-room. When he came up half an hour later, she pretended to be asleep.

In fact, it was hours before she slept, as the evening's bitter words replayed themselves in her head. What she needed –

what they both needed – was time apart, time to reflect on what was happening to their marriage and whether or not they wanted it to continue. But whatever else was decided, she must find herself a job as soon as possible. Andrew's taunts made that a priority.

On which decision she finally fell into an uneasy sleep.

The next morning they exchanged the minimum of words and it was a relief to both of them when Andrew left for work.

What she would really like to do, Helen reflected as she cleared the breakfast table, would be to work with antiques again. Perhaps if she wrote to her former employers? But she was out of touch with the market, needed more up-to-date knowledge.

She stopped suddenly, a plate in her hand. What about that course she'd read of, up in Broadshire? The place where it was held was near Steeple Bayliss; there'd be the bonus of being close to Pen, perhaps able to see her one or two evenings.

She ran upstairs and rummaged in her handbag for her diary. Then, sitting on the bed, she dialled the number.

Yes, there were still a few vacancies for the antiques course. No, unfortunately it wasn't a residential one; normally it would have been, but work was in progress on modernizing the bedrooms and they wouldn't be available till Easter. However, lunch and afternoon tea were provided and there was plenty of excellent bed and breakfast accommodation in the vicinity. If Mrs Campbell would confirm her booking in writing, they would send her a list of possible addresses.

It wasn't until she'd replaced the phone that she thought of the Seven Stars. Why bother trying to find somewhere else when she'd been so comfortable there? And it was only a twenty-minute drive from Melbray.

Ten minutes later she had spoken to a surprised Stella Cain, who confirmed that of course they'd be delighted to put her up for two weeks from Sunday the twenty-third. Remembering the interesting company, the good food and the pretty, poppy-splashed bedroom, Helen felt a grain of comfort.

She was tempted to ring her daughter, but decided against it. Since her plans would fuel more antagonism, it was better not to mention them to anyone till nearer the time. In the meantime, to lessen Andrew's cause for complaint, she would cook and freeze one-portion meals for the two weeks she was away.

With the decision made, Helen felt immediately better and the day passed pleasantly enough as she planned her cooking and freezing programme. Andrew, too, must have resolved to put the row finally behind him. He returned that evening with a box of chocolates, and though no reference was made to the night before, Helen accepted it as a tacit acknowledgement of his overreaction. For the moment life had teetered back on to a more or less even keel.

'Chris?'

'Hello, Dave.'

'I'm just phoning to see how things are going on the hit-and-run.'

'Slowly. There were flakes of paint on some tree-roots at the scene and broken glass from a headlight, but as yet we haven't pinned down the car they came from.'

'Any more on the girl?'

'Well, as you know, she was local, from Marlton. Ironically enough, she worked at the guesthouse where Skinner went to phone.'

'She was never walking home from there? It's a good three miles, and on a night like that −'

'She usually cycled, according to her parents, but that night she left her bike behind − probably felt it was too foggy to ride.'

'It would have been better than walking − at least she'd have had a light. But you'd think in that weather her employers would have run her home. What did they have to say about it?'

'Very shocked, as you'd expect, specially since under normal circumstances it wouldn't have happened; she usually

40

worked mornings, but that day she'd had a dental appointment so switched to the afternoon. Probably didn't realize the fog had come down till she was actually leaving.'

Webb grunted and changed the subject. 'Did you get to the exhibition?'

'Not a chance, though Janet went along one afternoon. Said it was very striking.'

'Well, it might come to Shillingham yet.'

A smile came into Ledbetter's voice. 'Oh, I doubt if they'll take it out to the sticks!'

There was a centuries-old rivalry between the two towns, now principally maintained by their football teams. Originally Steeple Bayliss had been the county capital, till increasing industrialization made its position in the topmost corner of Broadshire less convenient than central Shillingham.

'Well, any time you feel like slumming, come over and I'll buy you a pint.'

'I'll hold you to that. See you.'

'See you,' Webb replied, replacing the phone.

'It's your weekend off, isn't it, Dave?' Crombie commented from across the office. 'Anything lined up?'

'No; in this weather it's scarcely worth making an effort.' He glanced through the window at the dank, drear day. Though had Hannah been free, it would have been different.

'I'll probably have a painting binge,' he said. 'I've one or two ideas brewing.'

'Missed out on seeing the Russians, so you'll produce your own?' Crombie suggested with a grin. 'Fair enough.'

The Governor's artistic talents, though he rarely spoke of them, were well known at Carrington Street station. More particularly, they had several times been instrumental in his solving a case, the startlingly lifelike caricatures of the people involved alerting him to some previously unnoticed trait which proved significant. The process was known among his colleagues as the Governor 'drawing conclusions'.

What they did not know was that Webb was also the acclaimed cartoonist whose work appeared sporadically in the *Broadshire News*, signed by an enigmatic 'S' in a circle, denoting a spider in a web. He had a few in his desk drawer, he thought now; might as well get them off to Mike Romilly before he started nagging again.

With a sigh, he returned to his paperwork.

Hatherley Hall, the home of the Rudges, was on the north-east fringe of Shillingham, in the residential district of the same name. Since Charles also lived in that direction, Hannah had suggested meeting him there, but he'd insisted on calling for her.

It was another misty evening, streetlamps festooned with fuzzy haloes and everything damp to the touch. Hannah settled into the soft leather car-seat and pulled up her collar. To think she might have been in Paris with David!

The Hall stood on a rise of ground at the end of a long, curving drive. Through the mist, she was conscious of the tall, silent forms of trees on either side, like watchful sentinels waiting in the shadows. Then, round the final bend, the house came into sight, its lights struggling to shine out in welcome.

Charles parked on the broad sweep of gravel alongside the cars of earlier arrivals and, his hand at her elbow, they walked quickly to the door and were ushered inside.

As always on these occasions, the great double doors leading to both drawing- and dining-rooms had been folded back, making the hall into one vast reception area. A maid was waiting to take their coats, and at the top of the sweeping staircase a string quartet had already started to play. Things were done in style at Hatherley, Hannah reflected.

Their host and hostess hurried forward to greet them, and as she kissed Lady Ursula's papery cheek, Hannah thought, as she always did, how beautiful she must have been as a young woman. The delicate bone structure was still discernible, the eyes, though deeper in their sockets, were still large and lustrous, while her soft grey hair coiled into a loose chignon, giving her an air of almost regal dignity.

Sir Clifford was, as always, briskly charming in his immaculate dinner jacket, his thick white hair parted with care. The ebony cane on which he relied to ease an old leg injury was as much a part of him as the military-style moustache which now brushed her cheek.

'My dear Hannah, how pleasant this is! Too bad Gwen can't be with us this year.'

'I'm sure Canada has its compensations!' Lady Ursula murmured. 'Have you heard from her lately?'

'Not since Christmas, but she's enjoying herself enormously.'

They were interrupted by the approach of one of the waiters with a tray of drinks, and as the Rudges went to greet new arrivals, Hannah and Charles moved further into the hall.

Since there were twenty governors of the school and each had brought a partner, there was quite a crowd. Many were friends as well as colleagues, in particular John and Beatrice Templeton – Beatrice, in fact, being Gwen Rutherford's elder sister, and her husband the school doctor.

Having chatted to them for several minutes, Hannah caught sight of Monica Latimer, one of her oldest friends, and, excusing herself, moved across to join her. Monica was the proprietor of Randall Tovey, the county's most prestigious fashion store, but it was her husband George, a local bank manager, who was on the school board.

'I hope you're coming to our preview on Tuesday, Hannah?' Monica greeted her. 'Wine and nibbles and a chance to see our spring fashions?'

Hannah smiled. 'You don't have to sell it to me, Monica, I'll be there.'

'Good. Admission by ticket only, don't forget. There'll be someone on the door to keep out gatecrashers.'

'A pity burglars can't be kept out as easily,' Hannah commented, glancing at Lady Ursula across the room.

Monica sobered. 'I know. There's no more news, I suppose?'

'Not that I've heard. I feel so sorry for them.'

'For whom, my dear?' Sir Clifford himself had come up behind her and slipped an arm round her waist.

'You, actually!' Hannah confessed with a smile. 'We were talking about the robbery.'

'Ah yes, an infernal business. I think we must accept we'll never see our wine-taster again.'

'And now this Victorian miniature has disappeared,' George Latimer commented. 'How much would it be worth, Sir Clifford?'

The older man shrugged. 'A couple of thousand, I suppose. George Richmond is very collectable; he was portrait painter in miniature by Royal Appointment, and the work was signed. Furthermore, being a collector herself, Her Majesty didn't often part with such gifts.'

'Would the frame add to the value?' Hannah asked. 'I read it was studded with diamonds.'

'Yes, though some were missing. Separately, portrait and frame would each be worth a couple of thousand, but at auction you wouldn't be likely to get more than that in total.'

'Well, let's hope the police catch them soon,' Charles observed, having joined the group in time to hear the last comments. 'For once, I'm glad I haven't a country seat!'

The evening followed its usual smooth pattern. Delicious food was laid out on the extended dining-table, wine was plentiful and of excellent quality. Sir Clifford made his usual brief speech, and was cheered roundly by his guests.

Before stepping down from his elevated position on the staircase, he added: 'And on a business note, may I take the opportunity of apologizing for my absence at the next meeting? I'm conducting a two-day course at Melbray, and though I'll be back on the Wednesday, it won't, I'm afraid, be in time to join you.'

'Will you go with him, Lady Ursula?' Beatrice Templeton inquired.

'No, no. He'll be away only the one night, and I shall be quite content here.'

'You won't feel –?' Beatrice's question tailed off as she belatedly doubted the wisdom of it.

Lady Ursula smiled. 'Nervous? No, my dear, I shan't. For one thing, the servants will be in the house with me. Anyway, one presumes the thieves now have what they want from us. They haven't been known to strike twice at the same address.'

People were starting to drift away, and Hannah nodded in answer to Charles's silent query. Minutes later they were gliding back down Lethbridge Road towards the town.

'Usual high standard,' he commented.

'Yes; they seem very philosophical about their loss.'

'It's the only way to be, isn't it? I think it's shaken them, though. Lady Ursula looks more frail than last time I saw her.'

Hannah was silent, unwilling to think how Sir Clifford would cope should anything happen to his beloved wife. They were known to be devoted to each other, possibly the more so since they had no children with whom to share their love.

Reading her thoughts, Charles said, 'It will be lonely for the old boy if she goes first. A man alone is a knotless thread, as I know to my cost.'

The hint of depression in his voice was so unusual that Hannah was taken by surprise. To dispel it, she said with a light laugh, 'Anyone less "knotless" than you would be hard to find!'

'Appearances can be deceptive,' he said quietly, and she dared say no more. She knew he had been lonely since his wife's death, knew too that he still hoped she would rescue him from that loneliness.

And she was fond of him, she thought sadly. He was charming, thoughtful, and very attractive with that lean, clever face and easy smile. She enjoyed his company and they had many of the same interests. Also, and importantly, he understood how much her career meant to her, and his active interest in the school would be a positive advantage.

And yet – and yet – he just wasn't David Webb, she admitted ruefully. As things stood, she had both Charles's friendship and her relationship with David, and she was selfish enough to want that arrangement to continue.

All the same, at the doorway of Beechcroft Mansions she didn't turn away when Charles bent to kiss her. It was a good kiss, like Charles himself. Fond, hinting at hidden depths but making no demands. She withdrew before it could deepen.

'Good night, Charles. And thank you.'

He smiled crookedly. 'For what?'

'For the lift,' Hannah said smilingly, and let herself into the house.

4

Andrew was whistling as he collected his golfbag from under the stairs the next morning. Helen watched him with a dry mouth. The moment had come.

'Have a good game,' she said, and as he nodded absently, added, 'I shan't be here when you get back.'

'Where are you off to?'

'Steeple Bayliss.'

He turned, frowning. 'To see Pen? You never mentioned it.'

'I hope to see her, but I'm going to attend a two-week course on antiques.'

'*Two-week*?'

'As you reminded me, I need something to do; this is the first step towards starting work again. Also,' she continued above his protest, 'it will do us both good to have some time apart.'

He was suddenly still. 'What do you mean?'

'Oh Andrew, why not admit it? Things haven't been right for a while. As long as the children were here we could disguise it, but not any longer.'

He said tightly, 'I get it: this is all because I blasted you about that phone-call.' His voice rose. 'Good God, Helen –'

'You see?' she said quietly, lifting her hands.

'See what?'

'How it is between us. We can't discuss the least thing without your flying off the handle.'

'You regard this as "the least thing", announcing you're going away to consider the state of our marriage?'

'I'm right, though, aren't I?'

'OK, so I have a short fuse, but you can be bloody infuriating, you know.'

'I'm not saying it's all your fault; we must both change if we want to go on living together.'

He digested that for a moment, then said more quietly, 'I wish you had let me know how you were thinking.'

'Would it have made any difference? Anyway, let's use the time apart to see how we feel.'

'You'll come home the middle weekend?'

'No, it's part of the course.'

'But you are intending to come back, in two weeks?'

'Of course.'

'Can I phone you?'

'It would be better not to, and see how we get on. I've stacked the freezer with one-portion meals; all you need do is put them in the microwave. You won't starve.'

'You're not – going with anyone?'

'No, all by myself.'

'When did you decide on this?'

She hesitated. If she told the truth, it would reinforce his idea that it was tit-for-tat. 'A day or two ago. Now, you'd better go – the others will be waiting.'

He eyed her doubtfully. 'So I'll see you – when?'

'A week on Saturday.'

'What shall I tell everyone?'

'That I'm on a two-week course. What else?'

He nodded. 'All right,' he said, and added, 'Enjoy yourself.'

Awkwardly, he bent and kissed her cheek. 'Goodbye, then.'

'Goodbye, Andrew.'

She remained where she was until the sound of his car faded into the distance. The die was cast, her bridges burned, the Rubicon crossed, and all the other metaphors she could think of. She just prayed she was doing the right thing.

Before leaving home, Helen phoned Penelope, asked if she was free for lunch, and arranged to pick her up about twelve-thirty.

48

'But why are you coming up?' she demanded, and then, fearfully, 'Nothing's wrong, is it?'

'Nothing's wrong. I'll explain when I see you.' And Helen firmly put down the phone.

Thankfully, last night's mists had cleared, and although the day was not bright, it was clear and dry. Her spirits began to rise. She had the course to look forward to, and it would be pleasant staying at the Seven Stars. The four owners interested her; she'd like to know them better.

By the time she drove on to the campus, she was feeling more cheerful than she had for months. Penelope was waiting outside the halls of residence, looking, Helen thought, the archetypal student, with her long hair and faded jeans. She scrambled into the car and leaned over for a kiss.

'This is a surprise! What's it all about?'

Helen reversed on the gravel and headed back down the drive. 'I've enrolled in a course on antiques and it's to be held at Melbray Court, just outside town.'

'I know it, we went there for a jazz concert. But what brought this on?'

'Well, I've been at a loose end since Past Times closed. I'd really like to go back to what I was doing before I married, but I'm pretty rusty and decided I needed a brush-up before applying anywhere. The course lasts for two weeks, so it should give me a good grounding.'

'How did you hear about it?'

'It was in the local paper the day I brought you back. Remember I told you I stayed over because of the fog? In fact, I've booked in at the same place again.'

'Well, good for you. What did Dad say about it?'

'He was rather taken aback,' Helen said lightly, 'but he knows I've been restless lately.'

'So you've left him to fend for himself?'

'If you can call it that, with a freezer full of cooked meals.'

Her daughter laughed. 'Bet he'll be glad to see you back, all the same.'

Helen wished she could be equally sure.

They lunched at a pleasant wine bar in the High Street and Penelope chatted happily about the first ten days of term

49

and the girl who was sharing her room. Then, pushing back her plate, she said, 'Now, tell me more about this course.'

Helen reached in her bag for the prospectus. 'The first week covers furniture, works of art, ceramics and so on, and the second's devoted to paintings. During the weekend, apparently, we visit a local country house. It should be fun.'

Penelope glanced at the sheet. 'Sir Clifford Rudge, no less. Remember how, wherever we'd been, we always had to be back in time for his programme?'

Helen laughed. 'The days before videos!'

Penelope handed back the brochure. 'It looks as though you'll be busy.'

'But apart from Saturday, the evenings are free and so is the whole of Sunday. I thought we might have a meal or go to the cinema, if it wouldn't interfere with your work?'

'Great; I've no essay deadlines at the moment.'

'Say one evening, whichever week suits you, and next Sunday? Decide what you'd like to do and let me know; you can reach me on this number after about six.'

Penelope nodded and slipped the note in her shoulderbag. 'Have you heard from Thomas?'

'The usual request for funds.'

'Already? I don't know what he *does* with it,' said the thrifty Pen smugly.

'Tries to impress his girlfriend, no doubt.'

'But we all go Dutch, that shouldn't be a problem. Did Dad hit the roof?'

'Actually, I didn't tell him.'

Penelope shot her a swift glance. 'Temper uncertain?'

Instantly Helen felt disloyal. 'He has a lot on his mind at the moment.'

'The Stately Homes business, you mean?'

Helen, who hadn't known what she meant, seized on the suggestion gratefully. 'They're having no luck whatsoever. Each time it happens, the burglars and their loot disappear into thin air.'

'They're probably sitting on things till the hue and cry dies down.'

'But it *won't* die down if they keep doing more burglaries; and it's almost two years now since the first one.'

'Poor old Dad,' Penelope said absently. She glanced at her watch. 'Mum, I hope you don't mind, but I'm due to play squash at three. I fixed it before I knew you were coming.'

'That's all right.' Helen signalled the waiter for the bill. 'I want to do some preparation anyway. I raided the library for books on antiques and paintings, so I could mug up a bit and not seem too ignorant!'

Having returned her daughter to the university, Helen set off, rather earlier than anticipated, for the Seven Stars.

Today, the High Street was practically deserted and, driving leisurely along, she was able to appreciate the charming haphazardness of its architecture, a reminder that this had once been a small market town.

Ancient Tudor buildings, their black ships' timbers banding the white plaster, nestled against four-storey edifices with wrought-iron balconies and mullion windows in a companionable melding of the centuries. Some, Helen noted, bore the names of well-known chain stores, but, with their modern fashions hidden behind historic frontages, ancient and modern coexisted in a unique blend of individuality.

Once through the town, she settled back for the twenty-minute drive to the Seven Stars. The road she was following was fairly high, and to the right, rolling downlands fell away, giving glimpses of clusters of thatched roofs, a church spire, and, nearer at hand, barns stacked high with hay.

On the left, occasional farmhouses edged the road, steep-gabled and in Cotswold stone, with tall chimneys which looked as though they'd been stuck on as an afterthought and notices at the gates advertising potatoes and onions for sale. Far away behind them, Helen could see the wooded slopes of the Chantock Hills. Her quick dashes along the motorway, she reflected, had given no inkling of the attractive countryside which lay beyond.

Then the Seven Stars came into sight and, turning into the drive which led round to the courtyard, she parked in the same place as before.

Ahead of her was a shoulder-high stone wall which

51

abutted at a right angle from the mews block to form the fourth side of the courtyard. Helen went to look over it. Beyond lay a sizeable garden, drab now in the dank January air, but, judging by its well-tended beds and neatly pruned shrubs, a pleasant place to wander in summer. Roughly a quarter of it was devoted to vegetables, which augured well for the cuisine, and at the far side of the lawn stood a wooden summerhouse.

Shivering suddenly in her thin jacket, she returned to the car, removed her suitcase, and walked round to the front door.

As before, it was Stella Cain who answered it. 'Mrs Campbell – welcome back!'

'Thank you. I'm sorry I'm a little early, but there's some work I'd like to get down to.'

'Of course. You can sit here by the fire, if the constant coming and going won't disturb you, or in the television lounge if you prefer. There's a fire in there, too.'

'Thanks, but first I'll unpack and have a cup of tea in my room. Is it the same one?'

'Yes, I'll –'

'Don't bother coming up, I can manage.' Helen took the key from her.

'Are you sure? Come down whenever you're ready, then, and make yourself at home.'

Helen went up the wide staircase, thankful that her early arrival had been accepted; she was aware that in bed and breakfast establishments, guests were not expected to hang around during the day. In fact, she'd been hoping to spend longer with Penelope, but she had after all given her very little notice.

The cream and red bedroom awaited her and Helen looked round it with pleasure. This time, she thought with satisfaction, she had personal things with which to stamp it – her travelling clock, the tortoiseshell brush and comb.

She switched on the radio and started to unpack, laying underwear and sweaters neatly in the chest of drawers. Then she filled and plugged in the kettle and sat down in the red plush armchair to enjoy her cup of tea.

So here she was, she thought, looking about her with satis-faction and a sense of surprise that she had so far achieved her purpose. Andrew, albeit reluctantly, had accepted her two-week absence, and with it the prospect of a more serious work commitment. Admittedly he'd seemed less keen to con-template the state of their marriage and so, for that matter, was she. Still, two whole weeks lay ahead of her. During that time a solution might present itself, but if it hadn't by, say, the next weekend, she would set aside time to consider the position.

But not now. Finishing her tea, she collected an armful of books and went downstairs, opting for the privacy of the television lounge rather than the open hallway. As Stella had said, a well made-up fire burned in the grate, lighting the gloomy room. The glass door to the garden room was closed.

Helen seated herself in an easy chair by the fire and switched on the standard lamp that stood beside it. Then, opening the first of her books, she settled down to read.

DCI Webb leaned back and surveyed the canvas in front of him. He had spent most of the previous day sketching out in the hills, warmly wrapped against the January weather. Today, in considerably more comfort, he was attempting to develop the sketch into a watercolour, though not entirely to his satisfaction. Shades of green were notoriously difficult to reproduce, and he was debating whether to wash over them and try again when the doorbell rang.

He glanced at his watch as he went to answer it. Four o'clock on a Sunday afternoon: Hannah, keen to regale him with details of last night's party?

But when he opened the door it was to find DI Ledbetter outside.

'Chris! Come in. What are you doing in this neck of the woods?'

'Hello, Dave. I thought you'd like to know we've found the hit-and-run car.'

'That's great — where?'

'Your Duke Street multi-storey. It's only been there since Friday, so they must have kept it hidden for ten days.'

'Well, things should start moving now. Is it too early for a celebratory beer?'

'I'd give my soul for a cuppa.'

'You're on.'

Ledbetter leant against the counter while Webb filled the kettle. 'It was stolen,' he continued, 'which is par for the course. Reported missing the day of the accident, from outside a house in SB.'

Webb put a couple of mugs on the table. 'Is it damaged?'

'Nearside headlight gone for a burton. SOCO have been working on it all afternoon.'

'Fingerprints?'

'Plastered all over it; let's hope some of them are on file.'

'I suppose we can be glad they didn't sit on it any longer; it could have stayed in a lock-up pretty well indefinitely.'

'I reckon they wanted shot of it. Thought if they dumped it somewhere, it couldn't be traced back to them – or him, if it was a solo job – or even her, come to that.'

'Since the car was stolen, my bet's on a young lad,' Webb commented. 'And he must have known he'd hit her – he'd have seen her at the last minute if not before. A theory was put forward that he might have stopped, seen she was dead and panicked.' Hannah's idea.

'But she wasn't obviously dead, was she? The young couple who found her phoned for an ambulance.'

'True.' Webb carried the two mugs through to the living-room, Ledbetter at his heels. 'Think there's a chance it wasn't an accident?'

'Always possible, but anything deliberate would be tricky in that fog. Like, how did the prospective killer know where she was, or which side of the road she'd be on? Personally, I can't see anyone crawling along in that weather on the off chance of finding someone to run over.'

'Perhaps they'd had a row, she stormed off and he went after her?'

Ledbetter was unconvinced. 'Anyway, it's a start, and about bloody time.' He picked up a mug and walked over to the easel, surveying the picture propped up on it. 'This the latest masterpiece? You're a clever devil, aren't you? I couldn't paint to save my life.'

'I'm glad my life's not dependent on that,' Webb retorted. 'There's still a lot of work to be done on it.'

They chatted for several minutes while they drank their tea, then Ledbetter put down his mug. 'I'd better get back for what remains of this day of rest. Good to see you, Dave; I'll keep you informed of any developments.'

As Webb closed the door behind him, he realized that he still did not know how Hannah's evening with Charles Frobisher had gone. Which, he reflected morosely, might be the way she wanted it.

When Helen came down for dinner just before seven, it was to find a crowd of people gathered round the bar. In addition to her four hosts and Michael Saxton, there were two she hadn't seen before, a small girl in her twenties with a tangle of blonde, highlighted curls, and a tall, loose-limbed man. He had dark, curly hair and deep-set grey eyes, which regarded her with open curiosity as she approached.

Gordon Cain was behind the bar, and smiled as he caught sight of her. 'Ah, Mrs Campbell – welcome back! Can I offer you a drink on the house? We have friends in for dinner this evening. Let me introduce Caroline Budd and Dominic Hardy.'

They nodded to her and she smiled in response, then turned to Gordon. 'That's kind of you. I'd like a sherry, please.'

The blonde girl pushed her own glass across the bar top. 'And fill mine up too, sweetie, while you're at it.'

'I hear you're taking a course at Melbray, Mrs Campbell?' Kate Warren commented in her husky voice.

'Yes, that's right. On antiques.'

Dominic Hardy raised an eyebrow. 'Are they a hobby of yours?'

Resenting his patronizing manner, Helen answered levelly, 'Rather more than that; I worked in a London auction house before I was married, and then at a local antique shop till

55

the recession caught up with it. Now both my children have left home, I'm hoping to take it up again.'

'Good for you,' he said lazily, looking her up and down. Again she felt herself bridle, but almost immediately he smiled, and any hint of superciliousness was lost in undoubted charm. He raised his glass to her, his eyes holding hers. 'Here's to success. May you and your antiques flourish!'

'Thank you,' she stammered, and was grateful when someone made a comment and she was no longer the focus of attention.

'I didn't expect to see you again,' said a voice behind her, and she turned to find Michael Saxton.

'Nor I you,' she replied. 'I saw the course advertised when I was here last week, but I hadn't seriously considered taking it.' She glanced round. 'Is Mr Pike not joining us?'

'No, he goes home to Blackpool at weekends.'

'A long way to commute, isn't it? Why doesn't he move down here?'

'Not worth it; he's only on a short-term project, then he'll be off north again.'

'And you don't go home at weekends?'

'No home to go to,' Saxton replied, and smiled at her embarrassment. 'Oh, it's not as bad as it sounds. I've bought a small watermill not far from here and am having it converted into a house. In the meantime, this is my base.'

'How long have you been here?'

'Three months now. I'll miss the standard of cooking when I have to do for myself. Perhaps I should also take a course, on how to vary my diet of baked beans and fry-ups.'

'It sounds a bit limited.'

'It is. My daughter keeps plying me with Cooking-for-One-type recipes, but frankly I'm not interested enough to bother.'

'Have you just the one daughter?' Helen asked.

'Yes, and one son. And in case you're wondering, my wife and I split up last year.'

'I'm sorry,' she said awkwardly.

'Don't be; we should have done it years ago.'

She was silent, wondering uncomfortably if this was a

glimpse of how Andrew might be, if and when they separated: lost, adrift, living out of tins. Probably so, she thought; the last time she was away, he'd existed on toast and cornflakes.

She realized Michael Saxton had said something, and looked up hastily. 'I'm sorry?'

'I said, what about you? What family have you?'

'Also a son and daughter. Penelope's at Broadshire University.'

'Hence your appearance last week?'

She nodded, but before she could elaborate the call came to go through for dinner.

This time, the long table was laid with crystal and silver, and tall green candles burned in the holders. Helen found herself placed between Gordon Cain, at the foot of the table, and Michael Saxton. Conversation was animated and general, the food excellent and the wine plentiful. More than once, she caught Dominic Hardy's eyes on her across the table and felt a flicker of gratified amusement.

Suddenly he leant towards her. 'How long are you here for? Sorry, I don't know your name?'

'Mrs Campbell,' Stella said automatically.

'My dear girl, I'm not going to call her "Mrs Campbell" all evening!'

'It's Helen,' she supplied quickly. 'Do please use it, all of you.' She'd been conscious, last time, of being the outsider, with the others on first-name terms.

'Fine – Helen, then. How long are you staying?'

'Till a week on Saturday – it's a two-week course.'

'By which time you'll know all there is to know about antiques?'

She said steadily, 'Obviously it'll be superficial, but at least it should get me back into the swim.' She met his eye squarely. 'What do you do, Dominic?'

He sipped his wine, surveying her over the rim of the glass. 'As the phrase has it, I'm something in the City.'

'You don't live round here, then?'

'God, no! I'd die of boredom!'

'Dominic likes to be in the thick of things,' Kate said

drily. 'He lives in one of those luxury apartments near St Katharine's Dock. The reason we're graced with his presence is because he drives Caro up to see her father, who's not well.'

'And while I'm here, I take the chance of dropping in to keep these dear folk *au fait* with what's going on in the wide world.'

'We were at school together,' Nicholas said, by way of explanation, 'though Dom was a contemporary of my younger brother.'

'How is Ben?' Caroline asked. 'We haven't seen him for ages.'

Helen sat back, letting the conversation wash over her. She felt tired and pleasantly relaxed, anticipating with pleasure both the antiques course which lay ahead and evenings such as this, spent over good food in interesting company. How lucky she'd stumbled on this place.

Thinking back to her last visit, she said into a sudden lull, 'Did you ever hear any more about the girl who was knocked down?'

The silence that greeted her question made her look up, in time to catch hastily averted eyes.

'God, yes,' Gordon said under his breath. 'That was the night you were here, wasn't it?'

'Well?' Helen pressed, idle curiosity submerged in a sudden need to know. '*Did* you hear anything?'

'We did indeed,' Nicholas Warren said soberly. 'She turned out to be a girl who worked here, on her way home.'

Helen stared at him aghast. 'Not Molly?' she exclaimed involuntarily.

Everyone looked at her in surprise. 'How did you know her name?' Gordon demanded.

In her mind's eye, Helen saw again the running girl and the large, pursuing figure of the man who called after her. In the circumstances it seemed wiser not to explain, and she made herself say lightly, 'One of you mentioned her last time. But how awful. Is she getting on all right?'

Stella said on a high note, 'No, she isn't. She was dead by the time the ambulance arrived.'

Helen went cold. So when she'd seen Molly, she thought sickly, the girl had been running to her death. She gave an instinctive shudder, then realized they were still watching her.

'How – how dreadful for you,' she stammered. 'I'm so sorry.'

'Yes, it was the hell of a shock,' said Gordon after a pause. 'The devil of it was that she was normally here in the mornings, but she had a dental appointment so she'd switched to the afternoon.'

There was a brief silence, broken by Kate's calm voice. 'Well, if everyone's finished, shall we leave the table?'

With an undercurrent of relief, chairs were pushed back and everyone got to their feet. Michael said something to Gordon, and through the open doorway Helen saw them walk across the hall to the bar. By the time she herself reached the hall, the others had disappeared and Michael stood waiting for her, holding two glasses of brandy.

'You look in need of this,' he said. 'Come and sit by the fire.'

Obediently Helen lowered herself into the deep, winged armchair. He handed her a glass and seated himself opposite her, his eyes on her face.

'That girl's death gave you a shock, didn't it?' he said quietly. 'Why, when you didn't even know her?'

She was silent for a moment, staring into the balloon glass in her hand. She wasn't sure why she'd not mentioned seeing Molly – it had been purely instinctive. But, having not done so, she felt she couldn't now.

'It's just that I was caught up in the drama,' she hedged, 'when that man came to call an ambulance. I felt – involved.'

He didn't comment, suspecting, perhaps, that she was hiding something. Changing the subject, she said, 'Where did everyone go?'

'To their private sitting-room. It leads off the office,' he added, seeing her look blankly round for an appropriate door.

'That explains it. Are their bedrooms through there, too? There don't seem to be enough doors upstairs.'

'No, those wings at the front each contain a bedroom and bathroom – left side Cains, right side Warrens.'

'How convenient.' Helen paused. 'I suppose you've met Dominic and Caroline before?'

'Oh yes, several times. Her father's dying of cancer, so they come up quite regularly. In fact, as a long-term resident, I've met various friends of the family – and family too, of course. The Cains have a daughter living in Erlesborough and the Warrens two sons in London. They all drop in from time to time.'

'I gather the Warrens were abroad for some years?'

'That's right, in South Africa. I often wonder if they regret coming back. Nicholas fills in his time as a business consultant, which involves a fair amount of travelling, but Kate seems pretty restless. It's hardly surprising; she has a degree in modern languages and is a pretty high-powered lady. All she's doing at the moment is some occasional translating and faffing around here. It must drive her potty.'

'What about the Cains?'

'Quite a different story; neither of them has ever lived more than twenty miles from here. Stella freely admits Kate has the brains in the family, but she's an excellent cook and manages this place beautifully. She once told me she and Gordon were childhood sweethearts.'

'And Kate and Nicholas weren't?'

'No, they met at university, and according to Dominic, she was considered to have done well for herself, the Warrens being one of the best-known families in the county. However, that could just be Dominic being Dominic.'

'What a mine of information you are!' Helen said lightly. 'And what does Gordon do, when he's not behind the bar?'

'When he's neither behind the bar nor poring over his charts, he's a feature writer for *Broadshire Life*.'

'His charts?' Helen queried.

'He's a would-be astrologer, but at the moment he has to content himself with writing horoscopes for the local rag.'

'Really? He told me he was interested in it, but I never made the connection. I even read my horoscope last time I was here, but I didn't recognize him from the photograph.'

'I'm not surprised: it was taken years ago. How was the forecast?'

She laughed. 'Way out.'

'That figures. But the serious stuff is something different, or so I'm led to believe. Based on the time and place of birth, the position of the planets, and so on. And that's what poor old Gordon would give his eyeteeth to get into.'

'He could make a start with mine. I could use a bit of guidance at the moment.'

'Then ask him. You could be the first of an illustrious line of clients.'

'I might just do that.' She finished her brandy. 'Thanks for that; you were right, I did need it. Now, if you'll excuse me I think I'll go upstairs. It's been a long day, and I want to be fresh for the morning.'

He stood with her. 'Of course. Sleep well.'

It was as she was on the point of sleep that a snippet of conversation came back to her, which, subconsciously, might be why she'd not mentioned witnessing Molly's headlong departure.

Well, dammit, I thought she'd gone. God knows how much she heard.

Helen shivered, pulled the bedclothes over her head and determinedly went to sleep.

5

Gordon Cain walked across the courtyard to his study in the mews block. Overhead, the weak January sun was pushing aside the clouds and spilling a watery light on to the damp ground. He took out his key and let himself in, welcoming the warm blast of air from the central heating.

When they had bought the Seven Stars four years ago, this building had been virtually derelict, a mouldering store with broken windows, full of discarded furniture and cardboard boxes. Even then, he had seen its possibilities.

The block was divided into three, originally stables below and coachmen's quarters above. Nicholas had suggested knocking it into one building, to provide extra accommodation for family visits, but Gordon insisted that the end block nearest the garden should remain separate for his own use. Having never had space nor privacy while working from home, he did not intend to lose this opportunity and Nicholas, with no strong feelings on the matter, had shrugged and allowed him his way.

This downstairs space was a kitchen, with a hob where quick snacks could be warmed up without having to return to the house. It was furnished with a small fridge, table, chair and sink, and a cupboard for crockery and assorted tinned food.

An open staircase led to the room above, where almost the entire roof had been replaced by skylights offering a panoramic view of sky. Gordon loved to stand here at night, gazing up at the thousands of lights framed in the windows. Though modern charts meant there was no need actually to study the stars, he felt a great affinity with those other worlds spinning out there, worlds which, for him, no amount of space exploration could make any less mysterious.

His one great desire was to make his name as a serious astrologer, to have cabinet ministers and minor royalty consulting him before taking decisions. But gaining recognition was a long, slow process, and in the meantime the only outlet he had was turning out horoscopes for the *Evening News* while earning his living by supplying more earth-bound articles to the glossy *Broadshire Life*. He supposed there were worse compromises.

Today, though, he must prepare next month's batch of horoscopes, which were already overdue. He'd been putting off working on them because the portents were not promising; there was a whole cluster of planets in Capricorn, which could only mean trouble, and it depressed him having repeatedly to warn against negative influences in the daily columns.

Sighing, he switched on the computer and reached for his books of tables.

At Melbray, Helen, happily settled into her first class, was busy making notes. This morning was devoted to silver, and she was gratified to find, as the lecture progressed, how much she remembered from her time at Lamprey's. Several times, when the speaker invited them to date objects shown on the screen, she had been able to do so, and her fellow students were starting to look at her with respect.

There were about twenty-five in the class, mostly elderly or middle-aged women, though three married couples were among them and two younger women, who sat together on the far end of a row. There were also a couple of unattached men, one quiet and grey-haired, the other with overlong hair, flamboyantly dressed and obviously of some importance in his own eyes. He had not taken kindly to Helen's accurate dating, and she resolved to hold back for a while and not antagonize him further.

During the coffee-break, she heard him introduce himself to the lecturer, a woman from a local auction house, as Valentine Perry. From the way he announced his name, she gathered it should have been familiar, but it meant nothing to her.

At the end of the class, Helen turned to the pleasant-faced woman beside her. 'Do you know who that gentleman in the second row is?' she asked quietly. 'I feel I should know him.'

'That's Valentine Perry,' the woman replied, which much Helen had already gleaned.

'Should I know the name?' she prompted.

'Not if you don't live locally; he writes articles on antiques in *Broadshire Life*.'

'Then shouldn't he be giving lectures rather than attending them?'

'I suppose he's covering the course for the magazine.' They were now filing through the hall in search of the promised buffet lunch. 'My name's Rose Chalmers,' the woman added.

'Helen Campbell.'

'How do you do? I must say, you have quite a sound knowledge of silver yourself.'

Helen explained about her pre-marriage work at Lamprey's and Miss Chalmers was impressed. 'And you're hoping to take it up again? I envy you.'

Valentine Perry was already seated at one of the tables, and as Helen passed he treated her to a considering stare. She met his eyes with bland inquiry and after a moment his own dropped to his plate.

He regarded her as a rival, Helen thought, and was secretly flattered. Perhaps her knowledge wasn't as out of date as she'd supposed.

Kate said abruptly, 'What do you think of Helen Campbell?'

Stella looked up in surprise. 'I haven't really thought anything. Why?'

'Didn't it strike you as odd that she's come back?'

'Not at all. She's attending the course at Melbray.'

'I know that,' Kate said impatiently. 'But it could just be a cover.'

'A cover?' Stella echoed blankly. 'For what?'

'She gives the impression of snooping, that's all. The way

64

she asked about Molly, for instance. Did you mention her name in front of her?'

'Not that I remember.'

'I'm sure I didn't, so how did she know it?'

'She must have overheard it, as she said.'

'Also, she seemed upset on hearing she was dead; almost as if she'd known her.'

'Well, the accident did happen while she was here.' Stella forced a laugh. 'Don't start imagining things, Kate!'

But her sister was not to be deflected. 'Perhaps the police aren't convinced it *was* an accident.'

Stella stared at her for a moment, then picked up her knife and fork. 'I don't know where you got that idea. We answered all their questions and they seemed quite satisfied.'

'Only because they didn't ask the right ones.'

'Kate!'

'Such as why Molly was so upset she went running off without even stopping for her bike. If she had done, she mightn't have been knocked down.'

Stella said in a low voice, 'Please, Kate, don't bring all that up again.'

'Let's just hope no one else does,' Kate returned drily.

During the tea-break, Helen spied a copy of *Broadshire Life* lying on a table and picked it up. She started flicking through its glossy pages, and an amused voice behind her said, 'Page twenty-six.'

She turned. Valentine Perry was looming over her with a condescending smile. 'I beg your pardon?'

'Page twenty-six. My article. I imagine that's what you're looking for?'

'As it happens, no,' Helen said shortly.

'Oh come, you needn't be coy. I assure you, I'm flattered!'

'Without reason, I'm afraid. I was looking for a piece by someone I know.'

'And who would that be?' Patently he didn't believe her.

'Gordon Cain,' she said crisply, pleased to see his self-satisfied smile fade.

'Then I'm afraid I can't help you. I don't read his copy.'

65

And he turned and melted into the crowd. Helen continued her search and finally came upon Gordon's name above an article on the countryside in winter. But there wasn't time to read it before she had to return for the second half of the talk on antique jewellery.

As she entered the room, Valentine Perry studiously avoided looking at her and Helen was aware that she had made, if not an enemy, at least an antagonist. She almost regretted not pandering to the man's conceit.

When she came down for supper that evening, the local paper had been left, as before, on the small table in the hall. Helen picked it up and, now she knew the identity of the forecaster, turned with more interest to the horoscopes.

As before, 'Tomorrow's Birthday' was apart from the rest and she ran her eye down it, wondering to how many hundreds of people this forecast was supposed to apply. It was necessarily vague, with warnings about signing contracts and advice to concentrate on domestic issues during the year ahead. It finished with the innocuous comment that *a friend would like to hear from you.*

Which, Helen seemed to remember, was how the starred forecast had ended the last time she'd read it. She turned to her own reading, decided it had no application whatever, and dropped the paper back on the table.

Over supper, Stella inquired how her day had gone.

'I've enjoyed it,' Helen replied. 'Both the lectures were interesting and I was pleased to find I remember more about antiques than I realized.' She paused and glanced at Gordon, who, paying no attention to the conversation, was staring down at his plate. 'I believe you know someone in my class,' she said.

He didn't look up and Stella leant forward to touch his arm. 'Darling, Helen's speaking to you.'

He looked at her blankly. 'I'm sorry?'

'There's someone in my class whom I think you know,' Helen repeated. 'Valentine Perry? He writes for *Broadshire Life.*'

'Lord, have you been saddled with him? You want to watch your step, he can be spiteful.'

'I've already blotted my copybook. He caught me flicking through the magazine and assumed I was looking for his article when I was actually looking for yours.'

'You didn't enlighten him, I hope?'

She nodded ruefully and Gordon shook his head in mock despair. 'Then watch your back. He'll take it as a personal slight.'

Kate said impatiently, 'I can't be doing with people who take offence. Life's too short to have to stop and think before you say anything.'

'Although, my love, it sometimes makes for a more harmonious existence,' Nicholas observed.

Helen turned back to Gordon. 'Michael told me you're Stargazer in the local paper.'

Stella said quickly, 'It's only a stopgap, till he can get started as a serious astrologer. He has a real gift – people have already approached him privately.'

'But surely you can't be specific when doing mass forecasts? You must have to rely sometimes on time-honoured phrases like "Someone is waiting to hear from you."'

Across the table Kate drew in her breath sharply, and Helen found to her consternation that everyone was staring at her.

She said hastily, 'I'm not trying to decry it; it must be extremely difficult when you're dealing with large numbers. I only meant that phrases like that would probably apply to everyone.'

Stella, suddenly pale, again came to her husband's defence. 'Gordon's very conscientious, even with newspaper horoscopes. He spends hours up in his study, consulting the charts and checking that everything's accurate.'

'Oh come on, Stella,' Michael Saxton protested. 'With the greatest respect, Helen's right; everyone takes those things with a pinch of salt. How could it be otherwise, when one twelfth of the world's population is told to expect a letter on a certain day? The global postal service would sink under the strain!'

Stella smiled uncertainly and Helen flashed him a grateful glance. If she'd realized this was such a touchy subject she'd never have raised it. So much for Kate's disdain of people who took offence!

'No one claims it's an exact science,' Gordon said defensively. 'There are always shifting influences which can alter aspects. All we try to do is show tendencies, interpretations.'

There was a brief silence. Then Terry Pike made some comment on an entirely different subject and the suddenly fraught atmosphere dissolved; though Helen was disconcerted, on glancing across the table, to find Kate's dark eyes still consideringly on her. It appeared she had inadvertently blotted her copybook a second time.

Hannah was locking her front door as Webb came down from his flat the next morning. He waited for her and they descended the last flight together.

'How was the party on Saturday?' he inquired.

'Very good, as always. The usual fabulous food.'

'And company?'

'Well up to standard. Monica and George were there. In fact, I'm going to a fashion show at Randall Tovey's this evening.'

Webb made no comment. He had met the couple during the course of a murder investigation, which, he thought regretfully, was how he seemed to meet most people. Miss Tovey, she'd been then, a long-term friend of Hannah's.

Hannah, glancing sideways at his grave face, said contritely, 'I'm so sorry about Paris. Did you enjoy your free weekend?'

'I did some painting. And Chris Ledbetter called to say they'd found the hit-and-run car – here in Shillingham, if you please. It had been stolen, naturally, and there was no sign of the driver.'

'Perhaps they'll find something to give them a lead.'

On emerging from the front door they separated, Webb turning towards the garages and Hannah to the gate for her short walk to Ashbourne.

He hadn't forgiven her for being with Charles, she thought

as she started down the hill. But Charles was a governor of the school and there was no way she could avoid seeing him, even if she wanted to. Which she didn't, she told herself rebelliously. David would have to learn to trust her. At which point the memory of Charles's kiss brought a stab of guilt and, quickening her step, she determinedly put it out of her mind.

Sir Clifford Rudge was, as the class had anticipated, an out-standing speaker, and they listened enthralled as he sketched the social background to the artefacts shown in the slides, explaining that the fashions of the day influenced the style of furniture, and illustrating his point with the larger chairs introduced to accommodate the crinoline.

Eager to learn all she could from him, she was thankful he would be with them for two days. She would willingly have listened indefinitely to his cultured voice, soaking up the knowledge he so effortlessly imparted.

Valentine Perry continually tried to ingratiate himself with the lecturer and, though Helen knew the answers to several of the questions thrown to the class, she resolutely kept quiet. All the same, if the chance offered, she intended to have a word with Sir Clifford herself. He might be able to advise her on her hoped-for return to the world of antiques.

Webb had arrived at his office to be greeted with news of an attempted break-in at Beckworth House.

'They slipped up on the alarm,' Crombie told him. 'Thought they'd disconnected it, but triggered it somehow once they were inside. It's wired to Lethbridge, and as luck would have it, they had a car in the area.'

'Any sight of the villains?'

'Only fleeting. They fled into the grounds and presumably over the wall.'

'How many?'

'Two, it seems, but no description. It was dark and they were only spotted at a distance.' Crombie tipped his chair on to its back legs and regarded Webb over his spectacles. 'No saying, of course, if this is Chummie or just a copycat job.'

Webb said gloomily, 'Probably the latter; Chummie hasn't put a foot wrong so far. Was anything worthwhile found at the scene?'

'Not so far, though the SOCOs are still up there. The villains broke a small pane of glass and managed to reach in and unlock the window. Once inside they opened the French windows for an easy getaway, and had to use it earlier than planned. There's no report of anything missing.'

Webb frowned. 'Was there much in that room that they could have taken?'

'Plenty, from all accounts.'

'And they made no attempt to grab anything as they fled?'

'Apparently not.' Crombie paused. 'I catch your drift. If they were that particular, perhaps it was Chummie after all.'

'It crossed my mind,' Webb conceded. '*If* it was, perhaps this will give him pause, make him wonder if his luck is running out at last.'

'That'll be the day,' Crombie said caustically and, returning his chair to terra firma, pulled a pile of papers towards him.

6

Hannah always enjoyed visits to Randall Tovey's; there was a feeling of luxury about the place, and the assistants under the redoubtable Miss Tulip were efficient and helpful, reluctant to sell an outfit, however expensive, unless it was right for that particular customer.

In the foyer on this cold January evening a log fire blazed fiercely, and uniformed waitresses stood ready with trays of sherry glasses.

The normal displays of accessories – belts, hats, shoes and handbags – had been removed, and their places taken by chairs arranged in a semi-circle, with a printed programme on each seat. The models would, as always, descend the wide, shallow staircase, display themselves to the assembled company, and retire through the tearoom, returning upstairs by way of the back stairs to change quickly and reappear in another outfit. And afterwards, wine and canapés would be served in the upstairs showroom.

Hannah took her glass of sherry and looked about her with pleasurable anticipation. Such was the reputation of the store that the biannual fashion shows were considered part of the social calendar and invitations much sought after. These had been collected at the door by a uniformed attendant, and failure to produce one resulted in a polite denial of admission.

The smartest, and some of the wealthiest, women in the county milled happily about, greeting friends and discreetly taking stock of each other's clothes. Hannah nodded to the mothers of several of her girls as she went to join her friend Dilys Hayward. But just as she reached her, Miss Tulip took up a position on the bottom stair and clapped her hands.

71

'If you would take your seats, ladies, the show is about to begin.'

'Sounds like the City Varieties!' Dilys whispered irreverently as they sat down in the front row of chairs. Once everyone was seated, Monica Latimer came down the staircase, casually elegant in a lavender cashmere two-piece, and stopped on the bottom step which Miss Tulip had now vacated.

'Your Grace, Your Ladyships, distinguished guests, ladies. Good evening and welcome to the preview of our spring collections. I'm delighted so many of you were able to come, and hope you will have an enjoyable evening. If you have a particular interest in any of the clothes modelled Miss Tulip or one of her assistants will be available to answer your queries during the refreshments.

'Now, if you would like to refer to your programmes, I'll take you through the collections as the girls come down. And to begin the evening –'

One after another, the latest designs of world-famous couturiers were paraded before them. Suits, dresses, sportswear and ballgowns followed each other in a succession of dazzling colours, perfect cut and luxurious fabrics, ending, as always, with three or four outstanding wedding dresses. It was faultlessly stage-managed, and glancing round at the rapt faces, Hannah estimated Randall Tovey's would be several thousand pounds in profit as a result of this evening's entertainment. She might even succumb to one of the cocktail dresses herself, though she and Dilys had been invited as personal friends rather than customers.

Overheard comments as they made their slow way upstairs confirmed Hannah's impression of the success of the occasion. Monica stood at the top, shaking hands and receiving congratulations from her guests. Hannah and Dilys, who had arranged to meet her later, paused only briefly to add their own before moving to the long buffet table to fill their plates. Already the assistants were being cornered by prospective buyers anxious to make appointments for fittings.

Lady Ursula Rudge was sitting on one of the couches, a glass of wine in her hand and a plate on her lap. Hannah steered Dilys in her direction. 'Lady Ursula, how are you? I don't think you've met my friend, Dilys Hayward?'

The older woman's face lit with interest. 'The author? My dear, how exciting! I'm reading one of your books at the moment.'

Dilys smiled. 'I hope you're enjoying it?'

'Immensely. It's the one they did on television a few years back – I'm afraid I can't remember the title.'

'*Changing Times*,' Dilys supplied.

'That's the one – the family saga. It brings back my own girlhood.'

Hannah left them chatting and went to have a politic word with Christina French, whose daughter had caused some upsets the previous term. It struck her that Mrs French, as always impeccably dressed, was one of Randall Tovey's best advertisements.

It was crowded and hot in the upstairs room and the volume of conversation rose steadily. Nevertheless, Hannah was enjoying herself, greeting acquaintances, exchanging items of news and allowing her glass to be refilled by passing waitresses. Eventually, catching sight of Monica further down the room, she started towards her, intending to ask how soon they could escape to the Vine Leaf for a quiet chat.

But Miss Tulip reached Monica first, caught hold of her arm and pulled her urgently aside.

Hannah stopped, frowning. Something was wrong; the woman's face was chalk-white and against it circles of rouge glowed garishly like the cheeks of a Dutch doll. Hannah saw Monica gasp. Then she turned swiftly and, with Miss Tulip close behind her, began to edge her way rapidly through the crowd. Hannah craned to see where she was heading, and saw her push open the door of the ladies' cloakroom.

Someone must have been taken ill, she thought: then, with sudden anxiety, looked for Lady Ursula, who was no longer sitting on the couch. Perhaps she'd been overcome by the heat?

In her turn, Hannah too started in the direction of the cloakroom, looking about her as she went, and to her relief

73

caught sight of the old lady just ahead of her. She was shaking her wrist and holding it to her ear.

'Have you any idea of the time, my dear?' she asked as Hannah reached her. 'My watch seems to have stopped.'

'A quarter to eight,' Hannah told her, thankful to find nothing wrong. 'Is your husband calling for you?'

'No, he's in Steeple Bayliss this evening.'

Of course; the lectures at Melbray, which necessitated his absence from tomorrow's governors' meeting.

'Then how are you getting home?' Hannah asked. 'If you need a lift –'

'Not at all, my dear, thank you. Jenkins is coming for me at eight o'clock.'

Stupid of her to forget the Rudges' chauffeur. 'There's a quarter of an hour to go, then, and it's getting hotter and noisier by the minute. Would you like me –?'

She broke off at the sound of a handbell which Miss Tulip, still white-faced, was ringing frantically and which eventually cut through the hum of conversation until it tailed off uncertainly into silence. From the end of the room, Monica addressed the throng.

'Ladies, I'm afraid something rather distressing has happened. Mrs Stacey-Blythe has mislaid her emerald and diamond ring; she took it off to wash her hands in the cloakroom and when she turned back after drying them, it had disappeared. The room was crowded at the time, and it's possible one of you caught it up with your own things without noticing. I should be most grateful if those of you who've been to the cloakroom in the last five minutes could please check.'

There was a murmur of consternation and one or two women near Hannah obediently opened their handbags and searched inside.

'Perhaps it was knocked to the floor and kicked under a basin?' someone suggested.

Monica shook her head. 'We've had a thorough search and there's no sign of it.'

'What about the attendant?' asked someone else and, as

Monica prepared to vouch for her staff, added hastily, 'She might have seen something.'

'Apparently not.' Monica paused. 'Have you all looked in your bags? Or pockets, if you have any? The ring could have caught on rough material if someone bent over it to look in the mirror.'

'She's clutching at straws,' murmured someone behind Hannah.

A woman appeared at Monica's side, her face distraught as she caught at her arm.

'It's no use beating about the bush,' she said hysterically. 'Someone's taken it. They must have done. I insist you call the police immediately.'

There was a stunned silence, then an outbreak of indignant protest. Monica's voice cut through it. 'This is extremely embarrassing, ladies, but it seems I have no choice. I'm sure everything will be cleared up soon, but in the meantime I'd be grateful if you all remained here. There's plenty of food and wine left, so do please help yourselves.'

Dilys, appearing at Hannah's side, commented, 'Poor Monica – what a thing to happen.'

'It has to be a mistake,' Hannah said positively. 'It's just not possible that anyone here –'

'*If* the ring was taken, either deliberately or not,' Dilys went on, 'this could all be too late; several people have already left, and although they can be contacted, they'll have had time to dispose of it.'

'What's so disturbing,' Lady Ursula murmured, 'is that it must be one of us. It's not as though there have been gate-crashers; the doorman was most meticulous in admitting only those with invitations.'

Hannah said, 'I'm going to see if there's anything I can do.'

Monica was by this time surrounded by an angry throng, all complaining that their cars would be waiting for them and they had further engagements to go on to. Hannah went to her side.

'Please, everyone – I'm sure you understand how difficult this is for Miss Tovey.' Monica was known professionally by

75

her unmarried name. 'Your patience would be much appreciated. Perhaps some coffee might be a good idea?'

She turned to Monica, who nodded gratefully.

'Thanks, Hannah. Could you ask a couple of the girls to see to it? The tearoom will have everything that's required.'

Their better natures appealed to, most of the voluble ladies around Monica began to drift away and Hannah added quietly, 'Is someone on the door?'

'Yes, that was the first thing I saw to. But Hannah, most of these women are friends as well as customers. If they take offence –'

'They won't; when they've calmed down, they'll see there's nothing else you could have done. Have you sent for the police?'

'Tulip's doing it now. I just can't believe this. The evening was going so well.'

She turned as the Honourable Mrs Stacey-Blythe reappeared.

'I've been having another search,' she announced, her voice shaking. 'I keep telling myself it just has to be there, but it isn't.'

'Exactly what happened?' Hannah asked her.

'I took my ring off to wash my hands. I don't usually bother, but one of the claws is jagged – I've been meaning to take it to the jeweller – and I didn't want it to catch on the towel. I turned away for only a minute –'

'Can you remember who was standing near you?' Hannah inquired, aware of Monica's startled glance.

'No, it was pretty crowded. I'd been speaking to Mrs Ponsonby – she helped me look for it – but I didn't know any of the other ladies.'

'Would you recognize them?'

'I shouldn't think so, I didn't pay any attention at the time.'

Hannah glanced at Monica's worried face. 'Well, the police will know what to do. I'll go and see about that coffee.'

Inspector John Baker replaced the phone and went to the outer office. 'I'll need some WPCs to accompany me to Randall Tovey's. A valuable ring has gone missing.'

'At this hour, sir?' queried Sergeant Thomson, glancing at the wall clock.

'They're having some kind of function. The gathering is predominately, if not entirely, female, and body searches will probably be necessary. How many women officers are on this shift?'

Thomson consulted the duty roster. 'Penton, Crossley and Vane,' he said.

'Are they in the building?'

'I'll check, sir.'

'I want them in the car park on the double. We might need back-up but we'll see how it goes.'

'If they're at Randall Tovey's, sir, they're not going to be your usual type of villain,' WPC Crossley ventured as they drove up Duke Street.

'Which means a great deal of tact will be necessary. Nonetheless, if this ring *has* been nicked and not just mislaid, one of them at least is no better than she should be.'

'Definitely "she", sir?' queried Vicky Penton from the back seat.

'Definitely "she". It was nicked from the ladies' loo.'

They turned the corner into East Parade and immediately came upon a long line of cars drawn up at the kerb as impatient husbands awaited their inexplicably detained wives. Opposite the brightly lit entrance to the store, three wooden chairs had been placed to reserve a space, and as the police car approached, a uniformed doorman came forward and moved them. Baker slid into position.

Mrs Latimer was awaiting them in the foyer, pale but composed. Baker knew her from the magistrates' court, where she sat on the bench. She recognized him, and came quickly forward.

'Oh, Inspector, thank goodness you're here. This is all most embarrassing.'

'Has anyone left the building, ma'am?'

'One or two, before the ring was missed.'

'And none since?'

'No, but they're getting very restive.'

'Those that left, how long was it before the discovery of the theft?'

Mrs Latimer turned to the doorman. 'Frank?'

'A couple of ladies left together about half an hour ago, ma'am, and two others separately only a minute or two before you sent down and told me no one else was to go.'

'Any way of identifying these ladies, particularly the last two?'

The doorman shrugged helplessly.

'Do you remember what they were wearing, Frank?' Monica turned to Baker with a quick smile. 'Frank has instructions from his wife to report on people's clothes.'

'Well, Miss Monica, I do recall the last two. One was all in pink – I remember thinking she looked like Barbara Cartland – and the other in navy and yellow, with gold buttons.'

Monica nodded swiftly. 'I think I can identify them, if the need arises.'

Baker reasserted himself. 'Now, ma'am, how many ladies are up there?'

'About seventy.'

'Well, I'll come up and have a general word with them, take a look at the scene and so on. Then, I'm afraid, we shall have to search everyone.'

Monica's eyes widened. 'But Inspector, you can't! The Duchess of Hampshire and her daughter are here, and several other titled ladies. Whatever –'

'I'm sorry, Mrs Latimer, we have no choice.'

'But surely you need only search those who were in the cloakroom at the time?'

'It was crowded, I understand. The thief, if thief there be, might not admit to being there. Now' – as she started to protest again – 'shall we make a start?'

That evening was one of the longest Hannah could remember. The excited talk that had broken out after the inspector explained the procedure had given way to anxiety about the length of time required to search everyone, quite apart from the indignity of it.

There was a moment of drama when one middle-aged

woman fainted, causing the uncharitable suspicion that it might be a ruse to avoid being searched. Lady Ursula, whose chauffeur was no doubt in the long line outside, bore up reasonably well despite her air of frailty. Chairs had been brought from downstairs to implement the sofas that furnished this upstairs showroom, and there were seats for all who wanted them.

Having taken the police back downstairs, Monica showed them into the tearoom and watched while they organized themselves at a couple of the tables. At their request, she'd already furnished them with a copy of the guest-list, which she assumed would be ticked off as, one after another, the ladies submitted to the search.

'What exactly will be involved, Inspector?' she asked anxiously.

'Don't worry, ma'am, it won't be an intimate search. The ladies will simply be asked to empty their pockets and handbags on to the table and to unfasten their bras, which, as you'll appreciate, would be a convenient hiding place. They'll be asked whether they used the cloakroom this evening, and if so at what time and who else was there. Then one of the woman officers will quickly pat their bodies like when you go through security control at the airport.'

'You might as well start with me, then,' Monica said. She'd no handbag with her, and no pockets in her two-piece, but one of the constables ran her hands over her body, and she unfastened her brassiere and as requested jumped up and down. Then, with heightened colour, she walked over to the screen which concealed the entrance to the kitchen.

'I think,' she said, 'that last part would be less embarrassing if performed privately.' And she moved the screen to cover a corner of the room.

The inspector nodded impassively. 'Now, Mrs Latimer, if you'd kindly get them organized upstairs, we can make a start.'

The first to appear was a middle-aged lady with protuberant eyes and a large, tightly corseted body, who fixed Baker with an icy glare and stated, 'Young man, I might as well tell you I have no intention of being put through this indignity.'

A good start. 'I understand your feelings, madam, but I'm sure you realize –'

'*If* it's any of your business, I did not go near the cloakroom all evening. I demand to be allowed to leave at once.'

Baker sighed. 'I was hoping not to have to mention this, madam, but normal procedure is that anyone refusing to be searched is arrested on suspicion.'

'*Arrested*?' Baker thought for a moment the woman was about to have a stroke. Her face suffused with colour and she seemed to have difficulty breathing. 'Young man,' she spluttered at last, 'do you know who I am?'

'No, madam, though I appreciate there are some very eminent ladies present, and I greatly regret –'

'My name,' she stated, drawing herself up and glaring at him, 'is Lady Soames.' She paused. 'Did you hear that, young man? Soames. My husband is the Chief Constable.'

Baker closed his eyes briefly. 'I'm sure, madam, that he would be proud of the example you're setting.'

'Humph!'

So much for his chances of promotion, Baker thought bleakly. But to his surprise Lady Soames up-ended her handbag on the table without further urging, and produced a lace handkerchief from a pocket in her skirt. He nodded in answer to Vane's anxious glance, and the WPC conducted her behind the screen for the frisking.

'Well, I hope you're satisfied,' Lady Soames commented as she emerged, and, retrieving her handbag, she sailed majestically from the room.

'After that,' Sue Crossley said with feeling, 'the Duchess will be a doddle!'

The staff were the last to be seen, by which time it was after eleven. There were a dozen of them, including the weird old bird who'd made the phone-call, who gave her name as Hermione Tulip. Well into her seventies, her heavy make-up was of theatrical proportions but her hair, silver-grey, was smartly if severely cut and she stood tall and straight in an impeccable black suit. She was, Baker gathered, the linchpin of the establishment and appeared if anything more upset by the evening's occurrences than Mrs Latimer herself.

The models who'd taken part in the parade had, Baker gathered, left immediately afterwards and were therefore of no interest. Of the rest, the cloakroom attendant, one Daisy Phillips, was inclined to be tearful, convinced that suspicion lay heavily on her despite repeated assurances to the contrary. She knew the regular customers, and named several who had been in the cloakroom around the crucial time, which Sue Crossley checked against the relevant statements.

There were three waitresses, normally employed in the tearoom but brought in to take round the wine, and four sales assistants who had helped dress the models and stayed on to book fittings if required. And last came the three members of the catering firm, Home Cooking, who had provided the food for the evening.

In view of the eminence of the clientele, Baker was inclined to regard the staff as the most likely culprits. However, Monica assured him that apart from Mrs Phillips, who was on duty, they used the staff facilities and would not have gone near the first-floor cloakroom.

And when even they had been allowed to leave, there were the entire premises to be searched, for which Baker had requested back-up. When the culprit had heard the police were coming, her first instinct would have been to dispose of the ring, probably in the hope of reclaiming it later. The long showroom offered dozens of hiding-places, each of which must be searched out and examined.

It might also, he reflected, be worth SOCO's having a look at the cloakroom, though unless they proposed to finger-print the entire gathering – which heaven forfend, Baker thought tiredly – he couldn't see that much good would come of it.

While the search took place above and around him, he sat in the tearoom, accepted his umpteenth cup of coffee, and read through the list of statements which Vicky Penton had laboriously written down. The cream of Broadshire society, no less, but apart from Lady Soames no one had objected to their questioning. Nor, not unnaturally, had anyone admitted the crime. So where was the blasted ring, for heaven's sake? It seemed that one of those rich, highly bred ladies had after all had the last laugh.

7

Webb learned of the evening's events on his arrival at Carrington Street the next morning, where it was the main topic of conversation and where Baker's confrontation with the Chief Constable's wife had been recounted with more glee than accuracy, growing in unlikeliness with each repetition.

'She's a battle-axe all right, Lady Soames,' Webb acknowledged with a grin. 'Poor John – I shouldn't have liked to be on the receiving end.'

'His only consolation was that she kept calling him "young man"!' Crombie said. 'Naturally the press are having a ball. With all those big names, who can blame them? Jack says they're even asking if there could be a connection with the country house break-ins.' Jack Williams was the press liaison officer.

'For Pete's sake!' Webb exclaimed. 'At this rate, they'll be looking for connections every time a kid nicks a Mars Bar! It's obvious this was an opportunist crime and the villain a woman. What possible link could there be?'

'But all those nobs, Dave! It makes you think, doesn't it?'

'I'm glad it's not our pigeon, I can tell you that,' Webb commented and returned to his work.

Helen's chance came at lunch-time, when she spied Sir Clifford ahead of her in the lobby, for once unaccompanied. She quickened her step and touched his arm.

'Sir Clifford, could you spare me a moment?'

He smiled down at her. 'Of course, my dear. Let me buy you a drink. We lecturers have the use of a private bar – it will be easier to talk there.'

He led her into a small room off the hall, with large windows looking over the gardens at the side of the house. There were comfortable chairs and a glass and chrome bar in one corner. Two or three ladies were already seated at a table; in addition to their own group, a one-day seminar on lace-making was being held that day.

'What can I get you?' Sir Clifford asked, seeing her to a chair and propping his silver-topped cane against the wall.

'Dry sherry, please.'

As he went to the bar, Helen rapidly reviewed the points she wanted to raise, but first he'd a few questions for her.

'Forgive me if I don't remember your name,' he said, placing two glasses on the table and sitting down opposite her. 'Put it down to advancing decrepitude.'

'Not at all – how could you remember, when you give so many lectures? I'm Helen Campbell.'

'Delighted to meet you.' He shook her hand across the table with old-world courtesy. 'And are you enjoying the course?'

'Enormously. In fact, that's why I wanted your advice.' She quickly sketched in her background in the antique business and her hopes for resuming work.

'Well, my dear, it depends how much time you want to devote to it. You could take a year's course at the Courtauld Institute, but possibly in the first instance your best step might be to find employment at a local auction house, if there's one near you. Where do you live?'

'In Hampshire – not far from Winchester.'

'That shouldn't be a problem, then. Basically, what you need to do is study catalogues, walk round the sales and see how they're laid out, check on prices and get used to handling objects. Then, if you want to go further and qualify as a valuer and auctioneer, you could take the courses set by the Association of Fine Art, Valuers and Auctioneers.'

'Thank you – that's a great help.'

He reached in the breast pocket of his waistcoat and extracted a small gold-edged card. 'And if I can be of assistance at any time, do please telephone.'

She thanked him again. He nodded and took another sip

of his sherry. 'You've come from quite a distance; how did you hear of this course?'

'My daughter's at university in Steeple Bayliss. I saw it advertised when I brought her back at the beginning of term.'

'A pity it's not residential this year, but I gather they're doing great things upstairs – putting in more bathrooms and generally modernizing the place. Did you manage to find somewhere reasonable to stay?'

'Yes, I'm at the Seven Stars just along the road. It's run by two sisters and their husbands, and the food is excellent.'

'Is anyone else on the course staying there?'

'No, just two long-term guests and me.'

'Well, I'm glad you found somewhere suitable. I usually stay at the White Swan in Steeple Bayliss when I'm up this way. It suits me well enough.'

Out in the hall, the gong sounded for lunch. As they both stood up, Sir Clifford said, 'At the end of this afternoon's lecture I shall invite the class to come in here for drinks. I like to round off two-day seminars in that way. I do hope you'll come.'

'Thank you, I'll look forward to it.'

As they came out into the hall, Valentine Perry was passing the door and his eyes narrowed on seeing Helen with Sir Clifford. She smiled grimly to herself, then was ashamed for indulging in his own game of one-upmanship. When, therefore, he came and sat beside her in the dining-room, she prepared herself for more unpleasantness. But to her surprise he opened the conversation by stating flatly, 'You know Gordon Cain.'

'That's right,' she answered guardedly.

'Well?'

'No, but I'm staying at his guesthouse.'

'Ah. Then you also know his brother-in-law.'

'I've met him, yes.'

'What do you think of him?'

Helen privately decided that whatever her opinion of Nicholas Warren, the last person she'd share it with was Valentine Perry.

'Very pleasant.'

He shot her a malicious, sideways glance. 'At least you didn't say "nice".'

Helen smiled despite herself. 'I don't know him well enough to express an opinion. Why?'

'I just wondered what your impression was. He's quite a big name round these parts. His family were landed gentry, don't you know?' His tone was deliberately facetious. 'But to give him his due, he's a bright lad and he made all the right moves. Liked living in the fast lane, from all accounts, and being an ex-pat suited him down to the ground. Which is why I'm amazed he's not bored rigid, running a glorified pub in the country.'

Not sure why she was defending Nicholas, Helen nevertheless protested. 'It's hardly that, and anyway I gather he hasn't much to do with it. He does consultancy work which takes him all over the country, so you can hardly say he's buried himself.'

Perry, who had been eating rapidly during this exchange, took a drink of mineral water and with his next question unexpectedly switched back to Gordon.

'What did you think of Cain's article?'

Helen flushed, remembering her brush-off. 'I'm sorry to say I've not had a chance to read it.'

'You haven't missed much. You'd do better to read mine, as I said in the first place.' With which he pushed back his chair and left the table.

Helen gazed after him reflectively. Now what, she wondered, was the point of all that? But whatever lay behind Perry's questioning, it had succeeded in reviving her own curiosity about the ménage at the Seven Stars.

The drinks session at the end of the day was a pleasant occasion. Helen didn't attempt to approach Sir Clifford; she'd had a private audience at lunch-time and was happy to let others surround him now. Valentine Perry was monopolizing him at the moment, but then he did have a column to write.

She had forgotten Gordon's article until he'd mentioned it; she must try to read it tomorrow, in case Gordon himself referred back to it.

Idly, watching Perry chat to the old man, she thought over his comments. *Were* the Warrens bored with the life they now led? How had they really adjusted from what sounded like a glamorous lifestyle overseas? Michael Saxton, she remembered, had expressed surprise at Kate's willingness to settle down. What had made them decide to throw in their lot with the Cains and bury themselves in the country?

'You're looking very serious!' said a smiling voice, and Helen turned to Miss Chalmers.

'Sorry, I was miles away!' But only nine or ten, she added privately.

It was almost time for dinner when Helen reached the Seven Stars. As always, the evening paper lay on the hall table and curiosity impelled her to pick it up and turn to the horoscopes. This time, 'Tomorrow's Birthday' was not required to get in touch with anyone. He must change it sometimes after all, she thought cynically. Odd, the way everyone had reacted when she'd mentioned the column, as though they were on the defensive. She hadn't intended to sound sceptical.

'You're really hooked on those things, aren't you?' said a voice just behind her, and she jumped, turning to see Terry Pike looking at her curiously.

'Can't resist them!' she said lightly. 'Do you know anyone who can turn the page without reading them?'

'And what does the future hold today?' His flat, north-country voice made the query sound more scathing than perhaps he'd intended.

'I only read "Tomorrow's Birthday",' she said.

'It's your birthday tomorrow?'

'No, but – oh, it's too complicated to explain.'

He seemed about to pursue the subject, but to Helen's relief Kate appeared from the direction of the kitchen and summoned them in to dinner.

'I gather you got more than you bargained for at the Randall Tovey do,' Webb remarked, when Hannah visited him that evening.

'We certainly did. I felt so sorry for Monica, it put a pall on the whole evening. I suppose they haven't found the ring?'

'Not that I've heard.' He poured her a drink.

'Is there any chance they will?'

He shrugged. 'Information has been sent to local jewellers. If it does turn up, it could easily be identified – there are initials and a date inside. God knows why it was taken – it can never be worn in public unless it's reset. Why did the silly woman take it off, anyway?'

'One of the claws was raised and would have caught on the towel.'

'Then she shouldn't have worn it till she'd had it fixed.'

'Easy to be wise after the event,' Hannah said drily. 'Admittedly she should never have taken her eyes off it, but the fashion floor at Randall Tovey's is the last place one would expect to have anything stolen.'

'You know at least some of those women. Any idea who might have taken it? Off the record, naturally.'

Hannah regarded him with horror. 'I most certainly have not! David, they were –'

'I know who they were, love. The fact remains, like it or not, that one of them is a thief.'

Hannah said sombrely, 'And if she's never caught, we all remain under suspicion. It's appalling.'

'Did you go to the cloakroom yourself?'

She shook her head.

'Or notice anyone who did?'

'Not till after the alarm was raised. I was at the far end of the floor most of the time.' She paused. 'I hoped whoever had taken it might have hidden it somewhere.'

'So did John Baker. The place was turned over from top to bottom but there was no sign of it. Never mind, love, it might turn up yet. Stranger things have happened. In the meantime, worrying about it isn't going to help, so finish your drink and I'll get you another.'

The theft was also the main topic of conversation over the Seven Stars dinner-table.

'It's caused a right old hooha,' Gordon said, with his journalist's inside knowledge. 'Specially in view of the clientele. The duchess was there, for heaven's sake.'

'The Duchess of Hampshire?' Helen asked. 'We're going to visit her place on Saturday. When did all this happen?'

Kate looked at her in surprise. 'Last night, haven't you heard about it? I thought I saw you with the paper.'

'She only reads the horoscopes,' Terry said.

There was a small, taut silence, then Stella said quickly, 'Well, it was all over the front page, with a photograph of the store and police cars outside. Everyone had to be *searched*! Can you imagine?'

'How much was the ring worth?' Kate asked. 'Does anyone know?'

Gordon shrugged. 'Ten or twelve thousand, I think. Not megabucks, but enough to turn the insurance company pale.'

'And there's already quite a lot of pallor among insurance companies,' Helen observed.

'Oh?' Stella looked at her inquiringly.

'This Stately Homes business, I mean. My husband's firm is investigating some of the losses – they're astronomical.'

'I suppose they must be,' Michael agreed. 'Funny, insurance companies are the last people one feels sorry for, aren't they?'

'I couldn't agree more,' said Nicholas.

Gordon helped himself to vegetables. 'Anyway, how was your day, Helen? Were you able to avoid Poisonous Perry?'

'Actually, he joined me at lunch.'

'Lucky you! What did he want – to rubbish my work?'

'No, he was more interested in Nicholas.'

'My God!' Nicholas exclaimed in mock horror. 'What have I ever done to him?'

'He was saying what an interesting life you'd had in South Africa, and wondering if you found things dull now you're back here.'

'Kind of him to be concerned,' Nicholas said shortly. 'I

89

hope you told him I haven't yet succumbed to pipe and slippers?'

'I said you did consultancy work. That's right, isn't it?'

'It is, though what the hell it has to do with Perry escapes me.'

'He said you were a big name in these parts and your family was "landed gentry"!'

Nicholas held her eye for a moment, then burst out laughing. '"Landed gentry"? Do people still talk like that? It's what comes of working for *Broadshire Life*, I suppose; everyone's family tree is on file. You'd better watch it, Gordon, old chap, or it might rub off on you.'

The sound of the telephone cut across the conversation. Nicholas and Gordon glanced quickly at their watches, then at each other and for a moment neither of them moved. Both the women had also tensed and Helen, curious, looked at her own watch. It was exactly eight o'clock. Then Nicholas said, 'I'll take it,' and hurried from the room.

Kate, catching Helen's puzzled eye, said lightly, 'Why do people always ring during dinner?' She pushed her chair back. 'I'll put his plate in the oven.'

'Hardly worth it,' Gordon said. 'He'll only be a minute.'

Fleetingly Helen wondered how he knew that, but he was right: in a short space of time Nicholas returned and Kate duly retrieved his plate. What struck Helen as curious was that no one referred to the phone-call. Surely the natural thing would have been for Nicholas to announce who the caller had been, or, failing that, for one of the others to ask?

She shook herself impatiently. She was becoming neurotic about her hosts, looking for mysteries where none existed.

After the meal, Helen went to the television lounge. She wanted some time to herself to reflect over the day, and in particular the advice Sir Clifford had given her. But Terry Pike followed her in, settled himself in one of the deep armchairs and picked up the *Radio Times*. Helen expected him to switch on the set, but instead he commented, 'So your husband's in the insurance business?'

'Loss adjusting,' she corrected. 'Looking into false claims and things like that.'

'But also, presumably, trying to retrieve lost property?'

'Of course.'

'And, as you said, there's plenty of it about. Which firm is he with?'

'Hunter Stevenson. Have you heard of them?'

He nodded. 'He must have his work cut out at the moment. Has he anything to go on?'

She was beginning to resent his probing. 'Not that I know of,' she replied dismissively, hoping he'd take the hint.

He did not. 'Which of the Stately Homes cases is he working on?'

Helen flashed him a brilliant smile. 'Andrew's work is confidential,' she said. 'He doesn't discuss it with me except in the most general terms.'

Not quite true, but the nearest she could come to saying 'Mind your own business.' She was relieved when Michael joined them and, after asking their permission, switched on the television.

They watched the end of a programme on wildlife, the nine o'clock news and then the regional bulletin. And on this, the main story was the theft at Randall Tovey's – 'one of the country's most famous fashion stores.'

The owner, an attractive woman with fair hair, was shown talking to a reporter and confirming, unwillingly it seemed to Helen, that the Duchess of Hampshire and her daughter Lady Henrietta Wolsley had been among the guests.

There were one or two shots of the window displays and the interior of the store. It looked interesting, Helen thought. Perhaps on the way home she'd stop in Shillingham and pay it a visit.

'Things certainly happen while you're in the area,' Terry Pike commented. 'First Molly's accident, now this.'

'The police aren't sure it *was* an accident,' Michael remarked.

Helen swung her head to look at him. 'Why?'

He smiled slightly. 'They don't confide in me, I'm just repeating what people are saying.'

'But – what's the alternative?'

'Presumably either suicide or murder.'

Helen stared at him, distressing scenes and voices jostling in her head: the girl's headlong flight and the pursuer calling after her. Then, later, the overheard comment. Was that the voice of her killer, justifying his actions? *Had* someone followed her out into the fog and run her down?

That voice. She hadn't known any of them when she heard it, and even now she couldn't pin it down. To do so, she'd need to hear each of the four men in turn repeat the words: *Well, dammit, I thought she'd gone. God knows how much she heard.*

With a wash of horror, Helen realized it might have been one of the two here with her now. But would Terry have referred to the incident, or Michael reported the police's doubts, if either of them had been involved? Which left Gordon and Nicholas.

In her mind's eye she saw them at the dining-table, laughing at a joke. Impossible to cast either as a murderer. But then Andrew liked to say not all thieves had striped jumpers and bags marked 'Swag' over their shoulders. By the same token, not all killers had twisted lips and a gun sticking out of their pockets. Indeed, it was apparent from newspaper photographs that the most ordinary-looking people could, and did, commit the most heinous of crimes.

'Helen!' Michael repeated, more loudly. 'Are you all right?'

Her eyes refocused. 'Yes. Yes, thank you.'

He was looking at her curiously. 'Talk of Molly's death always seems to upset you. You *didn't* know her, did you?'

'How could she?' It was Terry who replied. 'Molly was killed the night she arrived.'

Was killed. The sinister little phrase repeated itself in her head, but it applied as much to a traffic accident as to a deliberate act. She pushed herself to her feet.

'I'm rather tired, I think. It's been quite an eventful day.'

Michael also stood, and after a moment Terry followed suit. She smiled vaguely at them both. 'Good night.'

'Good night,' they chorused, and were still on their feet when she closed the door behind her.

There was no one in the hall. The family must be in their private sitting-room. Helen went slowly up the stairs, her hand on the smooth polished balustrade. And suddenly, halfway up, she felt a great need to speak to Andrew. She paused, then turned and ran back down the stairs and into the corridor where the phone was.

Please let him be there! she thought, surprised by her urgency.

The phone rang for quite a while, then Andrew's voice said in her ear, 'Hello?'

A wave of relief flooded her. 'Andrew, it's me.'

'Helen! Hello! How are things going?'

'All right. Very well, in fact; the course is fascinating. What about you?'

'I'm coping.'

'What did you have for supper?'

'Shepherd's pie from the freezer. It was very good.'

So he wasn't existing on cornflakes, as she'd half-expected.

'Are you coming back at the weekend?' he was asking.

'No, I told you, I'm staying up here.'

'I thought you might be phoning to say you'd changed your mind.'

There was a short silence, and she realized sadly that they didn't know what to say to each other. She wanted to tell him she missed him, which was true, but she'd not had time to think over their problems, and daren't ask if he had.

'I'd better go, my money's running out.'

'Take care, love.'

'You too. See you soon.'

Helen rang off and stood for a moment in the silent corridor. Now the urgency had passed, she was wondering why, when she'd resolved not to phone Andrew, she had just done so. And reluctantly admitted the reason. It was because she'd suddenly needed to speak to someone who had no connection with this place, where she was becoming less and less comfortable.

Lost in thought, she walked out of the corridor and came face to face with Terry Pike. He looked startled. 'I thought you'd gone to bed. What are you doing, creeping about down here?'

93

Helen felt her face flame with anger. 'If it's any of your business, I was phoning my husband,' she said stiffly.

He made a small, apologetic gesture and started to speak but she turned abruptly away and went up the stairs to her room.

8

Helen was relieved that Terry Pike had finished his breakfast and left by the time she reached the garden room. Michael Saxton, at his usual table, had a small radio beside him, turned down low.

'I hope you don't mind,' he greeted her. 'I'm waiting for the overnight cricket score.'

'Then turn it up so I can hear,' she invited, and he smilingly complied. Though not interested in cricket, she'd no wish this morning for uninterrupted musing, and was glad of the distraction.

Stella came in with the coffeepot and filled Helen's cup. 'I'm hearing this in stereo,' she remarked, nodding at the radio. 'Gordon has it on in the kitchen.'

From across the room came the announcer's voice introducing the sports report and they all paused to listen. The England team was not faring well, and Michael muttered darkly under his breath as it came to an end.

'And now here's a summary of the news,' the radio continued. 'Reports are coming in that a break-in has taken place at Buckhurst Grange in Broadshire, the home of Lord and Lady Cleverley. It is believed that someone was seriously injured but no fuller details are yet available.

'The Prime Minister –'

Michael switched off the radio as Stella, murmuring something about toast, left the room. 'These break-ins are getting beyond a joke,' he commented. 'It's the first time anyone's been hurt.'

'Where exactly is Buckhurst Grange?' Helen inquired, her mind going to Andrew.

'Between Shillingham and Broadminster. It was in the news a couple of years ago, during its tercentenary. The Post Office did a commemorative issue of stamps, if you remember?'

'Vaguely,' Helen said.

'Well, Broadshire's got off lightly so far in the Stately Homes stakes, but they seem to be stepping up now. Perhaps it's to make up for the botched job at Beckworth the other night.'

'What happened then?'

'Oh, they broke in but somehow triggered the alarm and had to leave p.d.q. Escaped over the wall, apparently, as police cars came up the drive.'

'What with that and the Randall Tovey business,' Helen commented, 'the local police are being kept on their toes.'

With which sentiment Webb would have concurred. On this cold January morning he was standing on the terrace of Buckhurst Grange, his coat collar turned up and his hands deep in his pockets, watching the SOCOs at work. The point of entry had been taped and photographed and they were now searching the flowerbeds beneath the terrace in the hope of finding footprints. But for all the signs the gang usually left, Webb thought morosely, they might have dropped in out of the sky.

The crime hadn't been discovered till six-thirty that morning, when one of the maids had gone into the library to light the fire. And, in the best detective-fiction tradition, had found a body on the floor.

Except that it wasn't a body in the true sense, since His Lordship was still alive; though Webb didn't fancy his chances after lying severely wounded in a cold room all night. They'd not been able to speak to Lady Cleverley, who'd gone with her husband in the ambulance, but he'd been told the only object that appeared to be missing was a small porcelain figurine. According to the housekeeper, it wasn't particularly valuable, though it had been a favourite of Lady Cleverley's. Another of the 'cheeky' thefts, then, designed simply to show they could take anything they chose. But one which in this instance had badly misfired.

Entry had been made through the gun-room window. Webb supposed grimly they were lucky none of the firearms had been taken; they were all in locked cabinets, but that wouldn't have deterred this lot had they wanted them.

Sergeant Jackson appeared at Webb's side, interrupting his reflections.

'The butler says the household went to bed shortly before midnight. He locked up as usual and set the alarm.'

'Any chance he didn't?' Webb asked.

'You mean, might he be in on it? Shouldn't think so. He seems a nice old boy, genuinely shocked by what's happened and very worried about His Lordship. Blames himself for not hearing anything, but the staff quarters are at the far end of the building.'

'Was anyone else in the house, apart from the Cleverleys and their staff?'

'Not overnight, but they'd had two tables of bridge during the evening. The guests didn't leave till gone eleven.'

'We'll need their names and addresses.'

'I've got them here.' Jackson glanced at his pocket book. 'Revd and Mrs Arnold Stokes, General and Mrs Laxby and Mr and Mrs Anthony Silver. He's a consultant surgeon.'

He grinned at Webb's frown. 'Don't sound like a dangerous band of cutthroats, do they?'

'I'm getting Regional Crime in, Ken; they've got reams on the gang's MO and we need to confirm they're behind this. Specially since it could well turn into a murder hunt.'

'You don't think the old boy will pull through?'

Webb shrugged. 'A savage blow to the head, when he's well in his eighties? It's a wonder the shock alone didn't kill him.'

'If it was them at Beckworth, it would explain this following on so soon. Like getting back on the horse after a fall.' He paused. 'How many do Regional Crime reckon are in the gang?'

'Not more than two or three. No matter where the break-ins take place, the MO's identical.'

'They're pretty mobile, then. The furthest north was in Lancashire, wasn't it?'

'Yep, and the furthest east, Cambridge. They've taken their time getting to us – it must be two years or more since this started.'

'And in all that time nothing has been recovered,' Jackson commented. 'Quite a record, isn't it?'

'Depends whose side you're on,' Webb said acidly.

'Nice if it could be our lot that cracks it.'

'Well, we won't by standing around here.' He turned and started walking back along the terrace. 'I can't see that much will be gained by interviewing the bridge party, but we'd better make the gesture. There's a chance Lord Cleverley might have mentioned meeting someone interested in antiques.'

'What bugs me,' Jackson said, adjusting his shorter stride to Webb's, 'is why they take only one object, when they could get away with a fortune. Granted, what they do take is sometimes worth a king's ransom, but that ornament – it's just not worth the risk.'

'I reckon they take the cheaper things for kicks. Probably get no end of fun plotting and planning – Lord knows they've got it to a fine art. Not to mention making the police look bloody idiots.'

'But that china figure,' Jackson persisted. 'Did they go for it specially, or just pick up something cheap and cheerful when they got there?'

'I wish I knew, Ken,' Webb said heavily, 'I wish I knew.' And with a sigh he opened the car door and climbed inside.

In his office in Steeple Bayliss, Terry Pike sat staring thoughtfully into space. Then he pulled his phone towards him and requested an outside line.

'Pike,' he said curtly, when a voice answered. 'That woman I was telling you about: it seems her husband's a loss adjuster . . . I know; the last thing we want is someone queering our pitch . . . Hunter Stevenson, and his name is Campbell. Could be just coincidence, but check it out, will you, and ring me back?'

*   *   *

98

As Webb had anticipated, the bridge players had nothing to contribute but shock and disbelief. The first couple they called on, the retired general and his wife, were in their seventies and old friends of the Cleverleys. They were clearly distressed and Webb was reluctant to press for information. In any event, it was soon clear that they could recall nothing significant being said the previous evening.

'Of course,' the general added, 'we've discussed these confounded burglaries before. Bertie was naturally anxious, but the feeling was that all possible precautions had been taken. It never entered our heads that even if the worst came to the worst, anyone would be hurt in the process. It's the most damnable business.'

'Is there any more news?' Mrs Laxby asked anxiously.

'I'm afraid not, ma'am. His Lordship's in intensive care and everything possible's being done for him.'

'When you see Marcia – Lady Cleverley – do please tell her that if there's anything we can do . . .' Her voice tailed off.

'Of course.'

A similar interview took place with the vicar and his wife, who were in the same age bracket, but when they arrived at the Silver house, they found to their surprise that the consultant's wife was some twenty years younger.

'My husband isn't in,' she told them. 'In fact, he's at the hospital with Lord Cleverley now. He's a patient of Anthony's – that's how we met.'

She showed them into her sitting-room and offered them a sherry, which Webb declined.

'We wondered whether Lord Cleverley might have mentioned meeting someone interested in fine art, someone who could have had ulterior motives?'

'Not that I remember.' She hesitated. 'How much did they get away with?'

'One china shepherdess,' Webb said flatly.

Her eyes widened. 'That's all? It was for that that Bertie's now fighting for his life?'

'You know the ornament, ma'am?'

'Yes, quite well. It's a Nymphenberg – a charming little

figure but only of sentimental value. When I admired it, Marcia said they bought it in Vienna on their honeymoon. It could be mistaken for Meissen, I suppose, but not by anyone with specialist knowledge, which I thought these burglars had.'

'Occasionally, as you might have heard, they take things of little value – for pure devilment, as far as we can see.'

'Are you any nearer to tracking them down?'

'Up to now, they've left no clues whatever, but their luck might be running out. We believe it was the same gang that broke into Beckworth House and had to flee empty-handed. Now, there's the assault on Lord Cleverley, which I'm sure was unpremeditated. With luck it'll break their nerve, they'll make more mistakes and then we'll nab them.'

'The sooner the better,' she said.

During the lunch-break at Melbray, Helen was told there was a phone-call for her and found Penelope on the line.

'Sorry for the short notice,' she apologized, 'but I've managed to get a couple of seats for the rep theatre this evening. Would you like to come?'

Helen's spirits soared. 'Darling, I'd love to.'

'Fine. What time do you finish there?'

'The lecture ends at four-thirty, but what with chat and questions we don't get away much before five.'

'Well, come along to the uni, and I'll knock us up some pasta. The show starts at seven. It's *An Inspector Calls*.'

'I'll look forward to it. See you later.'

Helen dialled the Seven Stars and made her apologies for dinner, which were received without protest by Kate. At least she wouldn't have to face them all round the table this evening, Helen thought with relief as she went back to the dining-room.

On their return to Shillingham, Webb and Jackson stopped off at the General Hospital, which was next to the police station in Carrington Street. Lady Cleverley was at her husband's bedside and in the corner, trying to be inconspicuous, a uniformed constable also kept vigil.

At Webb's request, the elderly lady was brought to a side room, where he and Jackson awaited her. Someone came in with a tray of coffee and they all took a cup.

'Lady Cleverley, I'm so sorry to trouble you at this time, but is there anything at all that you can tell us?'

She looked at him with wide, haunted eyes. 'I knew nothing about it, Chief Inspector. That's what makes it so terrible. All the time Bertie was lying there, badly hurt, I just went on sleeping.'

'Has anyone been to the house recently whom perhaps you didn't know very well? Someone who might have been planning to rob you?'

Her face was blank. 'Was something taken? My mind's been so full of my husband, I –'

'A little china figure, that's all.'

'A figure?'

'A shepherdess, from the library mantelpiece.'

'My Nymphenberg?' She looked totally bewildered. 'That's all they took?'

He nodded. '*Has* anyone suspicious been to the house lately, ma'am?'

She made an obvious effort to think back. 'We had a musical evening just before Christmas. Quite a lot of people came to that. But Chief Inspector, if anyone was planning to break in, surely they'd be after something more valuable?'

There seemed no point in trying to explain the burglars' foibles and Webb changed the subject.

'Is your husband a sound sleeper?'

'Fairly, for his age. Occasionally, if he's restless, he goes down and pours himself a whisky.'

'Do you think that's what happened last night?'

'It might have been, though there was no sign of a drink. Perhaps he went down to get one, then heard a noise from the library.'

A shadow crossed her face as she visualized the attack. Webb said gently, 'What was the first thing you knew?'

'When my maid came running early this morning and said

101

he'd been injured.' She stood up suddenly. 'I must get back to him. When he comes round, I must be there.'

He didn't try to detain her. In the corridor he said to one of the nurses, 'Isn't there anyone who could sit with Lady Cleverley?'

'Her son's on his way; he's flying back from Brussels and should be here in an hour or so.'

Webb nodded. There was nothing more he could do here.

'Fancy a spot of lunch?' he asked Jackson. It was a rhetorical question.

Helen enjoyed her evening with her daughter. She had stood chatting in the communal kitchen while Penelope cooked spaghetti, which they'd eaten in her study bedroom, Pen curled up on the bed and she on the only chair. There was a bottle of Chianti to go with it and fruit salad to follow, and Helen had no regrets for the more sophisticated fare she was missing at the Seven Stars.

'How was the famous Sir Clifford?' Penelope inquired.

'Very charming and helpful. I asked him how I could get back into the antique business and he gave me some sound advice.'

'You're thinking of working full time, then? Good for you. And the digs are OK?'

Helen hesitated. 'Yes and no.'

'What does that mean?'

'Well, they're comfortable enough, and the food's excellent, but there are – undercurrents.'

'I thought you went back there because the people were interesting?'

'Oh, they're interesting, all right.'

'Then what do you mean by undercurrents?'

'It's probably my overactive imagination.'

'Tell.' Penelope settled back expectantly.

So Helen related seeing Molly's headlong flight on her first visit, and later learning she'd been the victim of the hit-and-run – which, according to Michael Saxton, might not have been an accident. And, with a self-deprecating

102

smile, she also told her about the horoscope column and how defensive they all seemed of it.

Penelope laughed. 'If I was writing horoscopes, I'd be defensive, too! I bet he gets the mickey taken out of him.'

'But I wasn't doing that!' Helen protested. 'I was only saying that sometimes he must have to fall back on generalities. They all have stock phrases and it's silly to deny it.' She paused. 'What about the rest of it?'

'Well, frankly, Mum, I think you're overreacting. After all, it was a foggy night and there were no pavements. Just because you saw the girl run out of the house doesn't mean someone killed her deliberately.'

Put like that, Helen could scarcely argue. 'You're right, of course,' she said meekly.

Penelope slid off the bed, collected the plates and carried them to the corner basin. 'Have you heard from Dad?' she asked as she started to rinse them.

'Yes, I spoke to him yesterday.'

'Is he managing OK?'

'To the manner born.'

'He'll be pretty busy, with more Stately Home burglaries.'

'The latest ones won't affect him; nothing valuable was taken from Buckhurst, and nothing at all from Beckworth – which, incidentally, is where we're going on Saturday.'

'It's pretty horrid, though, all these places being broken into, not to mention the old boy getting bashed on the head. And did you hear about Randall Tovey's? Pam's mother was there when it happened. She said it was awful, everyone having to be searched and interviewed by the police – even the Duchess of Hampshire.'

'She's having quite a week,' Helen said.

The Marlowe Playhouse was an intimate little place, resplendent with red plush and glinting chandeliers. Helen settled happily back in her seat, enjoying the rustling of programmes round about her and the general air of anticipation.

Pen was right, she reflected, she'd been letting her imagination play tricks. In future she'd keep it in check, and no doubt sleep better at night. Having reached which sensible decision, she settled back to enjoy the play.

'Hannah? I'm about to make you an offer you can't refuse!'
  'Surprise me.'
  'You've not eaten yet?'
  'No?'
  'Then let's drive out somewhere, buy some fish and chips soused in salt and vinegar, and eat them in the car out of the newspaper.'
  'You're out of date there; they come in paper bags nowadays. But what brought this on?'
  'A surfeit of the gentry. I'm awash with Lords and Ladies, Dukes and Duchesses and I need to go slumming. I'd like to take in some ten-pin bowling, but it wouldn't help your image if you were recognized.'
  'With that I agree, but I'm game for the fish and chips.'
  'Great. I'll be at your door in ten minutes.'

Friday morning brought the news that Lord Cleverley had died during the night without regaining consciousness. So now they had a murder on their hands. Furthermore, the weapon had been identified as one of a pair of silver candlesticks.
  Despite the seriousness of the case, the game of Cluedo kept impingeing on Webb's deliberations. 'In the library, with a candlestick.' All that remained was to name the perpetrator. Who was the real-life Colonel Mustard, Miss Scarlet or Professor Plum?
  He rubbed a hand over his face and reached for the telephone as it rang.
  'Someone's reported seeing a car in the vicinity on Wednesday night, sir.' It was one of the Regional Crime team.
  'Any details?' Webb demanded.
  'Dark, saloon-type. Not much to go on.'
  'Who saw it?'
  'A young couple walking back from a disco. Thought it was some lovers parked for a spot of nooky, but when they

glanced inside it was empty. We took them back to pin down the spot and got some shots and a cast of the tyre marks.'

'Excellent, Bill. Perhaps their luck really is running out.'

Although Hannah knew from David that there was no news on the Randall Tovey theft, she rang Monica later that morning to ask how things were progressing.

'They seem to be at a standstill.' Her friend's voice sounded strained. 'Honestly, Hannah, I've hardly slept since it happened. I just can't *believe* it. No one's going to feel safe in the store ever again.'

'Have the police been in touch?'

'Only with more questions. There's not so much as a whisper about the ring.'

'How about a spot of lunch, to take your mind off it?'

'I'd love to, but I've a rep. coming at two-thirty so it must be a quick one.'

'Fine. Twelve-thirty at the Vine Leaf?'

'Perfect.'

That Monica hadn't been exaggerating her anxiety was apparent as soon as she arrived. There were shadows under her eyes and fine lines at their corners, which Hannah hadn't noticed before. She joined her at the corner table, glancing through the glass doors to the courtyard which, in summer, was a favourite eating place. Now, the chairs and tables were stacked under canvas and a few desultory leaves skittered over the paving stones.

'I hate January,' Monica said.

'*When winter comes –*' Hannah quoted rallyingly. 'I was studying the blackboard before you arrived and the chef's choice today is *lasagne al forno*. How about that? With salad and a rather better wine than usual, to cheer us up?'

'Fine.' Monica waited while Hannah went to the bar to give the order. When she resumed her seat, she said quietly, 'Thanks, love. This is just what I need.'

'These things happen, and you just have to roll with them. Think of the problems I had last term.'

Monica nodded gravely. 'At least no one was hurt, thank God. But Hannah, I keep going over and over the guest-list, considering each in turn as a potential thief. And I know them all so well, either socially or professionally or both. I just can't believe any one of them would have taken it.'

'And you're quite sure about the attendant?'

'As sure as I can be. She's always seemed scrupulously honest. Now, the poor woman spends most of her time in tears threatening to leave because she's convinced we think she's to blame.'

'It was such a short space of time,' Hannah mused. 'One minute the ring was there, the next it was gone. It's not as though some time had elapsed, which would give a wider range of suspects.'

'Did *you* see anyone go into the cloakroom?' Monica asked despairingly.

'Afraid not. I was down at the far end most of the time.'

'And I was so busy chatting to everyone, I never even glanced in that direction. But those who were there seem to have corroborated each other's presence and you'd think would have noticed if one of them had grabbed the ring.'

'It's easily done. Someone could have dropped a hanky over it and scooped it up without anyone seeing.'

The wine came, rich, fruity and bracing, and by unspoken assent no more was said on the subject. They talked instead of mutual friends and holiday plans, and by the time the meal was finished, some of the strain had left Monica's face.

'We should do this more often,' she said as they parted outside the wine bar. 'Sandwiches at your desk have a limited appeal.'

Hannah smiled agreement. 'We'll fix another date in a few weeks. And by then, I'm sure, all the problems will be resolved.'

'In the meantime, thanks for taking my mind off them. Bless you, Hannah.' Monica lent forward to kiss her cheek, and Hannah watched her cross the road and start down the short street that led back to East Parade. Then, with a small sigh, she went to reclaim her car.

9

Saturday morning dawned the brightest of the week. There had been a heavy overnight frost which covered the cars with a sparkling mantle, and overhead the sky was a cloudless blue.

'I presume you're free today?' Michael asked Helen at breakfast.

'No, actually, but it should be fun. We're having a talk on Beckworth House, then going along to visit it and have lunch there. And this evening there's a competition followed by dinner, so I shan't be back till late.'

'Busy, busy. A pity you'll be indoors, though, on such a lovely day.'

'We have the afternoon free, to look round the gardens.' She paused. 'What are you doing?'

'I shall go and see how the house is coming along. Actually, I was going to invite you to join me. You might find it quite interesting.'

'Oh, Michael, I'm sorry. I should have loved to.'

'Never mind. I'll give my daughter a ring, on the off chance that she's not fully booked up for the weekend.'

He sounded lonely, Helen thought, and wondered suddenly if Andrew was, also. But no, she told herself almost at once. He'll be off playing golf and won't miss her at all, except perhaps when he has to thaw and reheat his own supper.

She said, 'Haven't you any friends in the area?'

'Not really. I'm not a clubbable man and though they're pleasant enough at the office, there's no one I'd particularly like to spend my spare time with. Once I'm in the house, of course, there'll be plenty to do.'

She folded her napkin. 'Well, I'd better be on my way. Tell me about it tomorrow.'

He nodded and, feeling she was deserting him, she collected her things and set off for Melbray.

The group had gathered in the usual lecture room, and Melissa Tidy was ticking off new arrivals on her list. It was she who was responsible for the overall running of the course, to whom Helen had originally spoken on the phone and who had confirmed her booking. She was a small, neat woman of about forty, with smooth dark hair tucked behind her ears.

The chairs, normally arranged in rows, had been grouped more informally round the room and coffee was being served. Helen sat, as usual, with Miss Chalmers.

Once they had all arrived, 'Melissa', as she asked them to call her, began to outline the day ahead. 'A coach is collecting us at ten-thirty for the drive to Beckworth, which takes about an hour and a half. We'll be driving through some of the loveliest countryside in the area, and up into the Chantock Hills. I shall, of course, point out places of interest as we go.

'As you know, the House isn't open to the public at this time of year, so we'll have it to ourselves. The tour will be conducted by one of the official guides and will take about an hour, after which we shall have a private lunch in the Orangery at approximately one o'clock.

'You will then have roughly two hours to look round the grounds. Do try to see the lily pond; it's in a lovely setting and well worth a visit even without its flowers. It also has the dubious distinction of having featured in a murder case last spring, as you might have heard. Then there's the folly and a maze and some very interesting statuary.'

She lapsed into what Helen considered 'brochure-speak'. 'Beckworth House has been the country seat of the Dukes of Hampshire for the last five hundred years, though the original building was destroyed by fire in 1680. The present one took over forty years to complete and is an early example of the great Palladian country houses. It has many fine antiques and an enviable collection of Louis XV furniture.'

A brief description of the contents of the house ensued, followed by a potted history of the Hampshires, who had

108

had their share of eccentrics over the years. One duke was apt to hide in the shrubbery and take pot shots at visitors; another cast a too-familiar eye at the Virgin Queen and only just escaped the Tower.

The coach arrived promptly and they filed out to it. Helen took a window seat and was keeping an eye open for Miss Chalmers, who'd gone back for her camera, when to her startled surprise Valentine Perry plonked himself down beside her.

She opened her mouth to protest, then closed it again. It would please him to know he'd disconcerted her and he was unlikely in any case to vacate his seat. But an hour and a half of him! she thought despairingly.

The first part of the trip was familiar ground, and a few minutes later they were passing the Seven Stars. Perry, seeing her glance at it, said reflectively, 'An odd bloke, Cain. Fancies himself as an astrologer. Did you know?'

Unwilling to encourage him, she merely nodded.

'Not much good, if you ask me. I have a pal who works on the *Evening News* and he says the man's a pest, always wanting to add things at the last minute. If he wasn't in with the editor, he'd never have lasted this long.'

Interested in spite of herself, Helen turned her head. 'How do you mean, add things?'

'Well, he has to submit a month's supply of horoscopes two weeks ahead of the first publication, i.e. halfway through the previous month. He manages that all right, but then can't leave well alone and keeps wanting to embellish bits.'

Helen frowned. 'In what way?'

'By sticking sentences on the end. Dick says that what really bugs him is that it's never anything earth-shattering, just more of the same drivel – *Someone is waiting to hear from you* and suchlike. I mean, what the hell difference does it make? It's not as though anyone *believes* the things.'

Helen felt a prick of excitement. She said carefully, 'But doesn't it alter the setting of the column, adding something at the last minute?' And waited tensely for his reply.

'No, because for some reason it's always "Tomorrow's Birthday" he goes for, which is in a separate box.'

She slowly released her breath. She'd been right, then. There *was* something peculiar about the horoscope column. Was it being used to send coded messages? But that was ridiculous: this wasn't wartime, with the country full of spies, and what was wrong with the telephone? Penelope's voice repeated in her head, 'Frankly, Mum, I think you're over-reacting.'

But the phrase Perry had quoted as a typical addition was the very one she'd challenged Gordon with at the dinner-table, with such uncomfortable results. Coincidence? Or had she unwittingly stumbled on to something?

The switching on of the tannoy made her jump. Melissa was beginning to describe the market town of Marlton which they were now approaching and which had been mentioned in the Domesday Book. Everyone dutifully looked out of the windows at the old market cross, the thatched cottages and cobbled streets, and heard how it had been held in siege by Cromwell's men because the King was thought to be hiding there.

Perry had lapsed into silence, either listening to the spiel or busy with his own thoughts, and Helen was grateful. Her own mind was only half on the history of Broadshire which was being recounted for her benefit. The other half worried at his revelations about the horoscopes. If a message *was* being passed on, who was it intended for, and how was a reply received?

Deciding finally that the whole thing was much too far-fetched and that she was once again letting her imagination run riot, Helen put it all firmly out of her mind and determined to enjoy her day.

Webb was sitting in his office, dispiritedly reading through the negative information gleaned by the SOCOs at Buckhurst Grange, when the phone rang and he lifted it to find Chris Ledbetter on the line.

'Just to let you know we've nabbed the driver of the hit-and-run vehicle. As we suspected, a lad in his teens who nicked the car for a dare.'

'Did he know he'd hit her?'

'Yep, but he panicked and drove on.'

'He could at least have phoned for an ambulance,' Webb said disgustedly.

'That's what'll count against him, but at least it confirms the death wasn't deliberate.'

'Never really thought it was, did we? How did you get on to him?'

'His father brought him in. He's been in a state, apparently, ever since hearing the girl was dead, and his dad finally wheedled the story out of him. I reckon he's had a good thrashing, though nothing was said.'

Webb grunted. 'Well, we've another death on our hands now, and there's no doubt this one was deliberate – or at least, the GBH was.'

'No leads, I suppose?'

'Not that you'd notice. All SOCO came up with were a few minute hairs. The DNA doesn't tie in with any of the family, but until we have some to match them with, we're no better off. God knows, Chris, we've been getting enough stick for not sussing out these robberies, but now a murder's thrown in, the heat's really on and we still have damn-all to go on.'

'Regional Crime helping out?'

'Yes, they sent a team over, but though we're awash with statistics and comparisons, they've not done us much good. The only light on the horizon is that a car was spotted nearby, but the description's pretty vague and it'll take a hell of a lot of finding.'

'Well, good luck. I'll keep in touch.'

'We'll need it,' Webb said under his breath, and returned to his papers.

In his sunny studio in the stable block, Gordon Cain was also experiencing frustration, compounded by a growing sense of unease. Depressed by general negative influences, he'd called up his own chart, only to be reminded that Venus and Mars were in opposition. Strained relationships all round, no doubt, which recent events had already foreshadowed.

He stood up, running his hand distractedly through his hair. It was one of his most basic beliefs that astrology gave warning of difficulties ahead so that evading action might be taken. The trouble was, he'd not the remotest idea what action he could take. It was as though bad luck – or, more technically, inauspicious influences – were bearing steadily down on him like an avalanche and there was nowhere he could hide.

Not that it had come out of the blue, he reminded himself. He progressed his own and Stella's charts regularly, and this period of strain had been approaching for some time. But things had been going so well for so long now that he'd become complacent, confident he could ward off its more serious implications. Now, his confidence had evaporated and for the first time he felt afraid.

The coach decanted them in the car park alongside the western wall of the estate, and in twos and threes the party made their way to the entrance. A small gate, inset in the huge ornamental ones, stood open and a smiling woman was waiting inside.

'Welcome to Beckworth House,' she greeted them, as they filed in. 'I'm Alison Carey, and I'll be your guide on the tour.'

Under the tall cedars frost still rimed the grass, but it had melted from the drive which wound up to the house. Helen noted the various paths that led off, signposted 'Maze' and 'Folly' and 'Walled Garden'. This place would be gorgeous in summer, she thought. Then, as they rounded the last curve of the drive, the house lay before them, its honey-coloured stone glowing in the winter sunshine.

'Isn't it lovely?' she exclaimed involuntarily, and Mrs Carey smiled at her.

'Yes, it is. Even though I live at the Lodge and see it every day, it always gives me a lift. Now,' she turned as the last stragglers caught up with them, 'if you're all ready, we'll go inside. Since we're such a small number, we can be quite informal, so do please ask me as we go round, if there's anything you want to know.'

They passed through the Palladian entrance into the Great Hall where, on a table to one side, a selection of guide books and postcards were laid out. Mrs Carey held up a glossy brochure resplendent with colour photographs of the rooms they were about to see.

'If you want a souvenir of your visit, may I suggest you buy one of these? Unfortunately, in view of the rising number of burglaries from Stately Homes, we've had to ban the use of cameras inside the house. We know thieves use photographs to plan raids, and as you might have heard, we had an attempted break-in the other day. I'm sure you'll understand that we must keep to the rule, even with private parties.'

'And it's also good for business!' Valentine Perry murmured in Helen's ear as they obediently queued at the table.

After some comments on the Hall in which they stood and the family portraits that lined it, they proceeded to the Library, a dark room whose walls were entirely lined with books. It was dominated by a huge desk on which stood several signed photographs of the Royal Family in silver frames and a display of enamel snuff-boxes.

Then came the Gold Drawing Room and the Dining Room, with its famous Louis XV chairs and a long table resplendently laid with a Meissen dinner service and tall crystal glasses. This room, Mrs Carey informed them, could be hired for wedding receptions and private parties, a way, no doubt, of offsetting the ever-increasing costs of running a country estate.

And everywhere there were urns, vases and jardinières filled with flowers, grown in the greenhouses on the estate. In the middle of winter, these seemed to Helen even more luxurious than the gold plate.

The Music Room housed a collection of ancient instruments; the Breakfast Room, decorated in green and gold, a cabinet of early Broadshire porcelain, with its distinctive gold and silver scrolling. Helen, bemused by the splendour and despairing of remembering even half the facts and dates which Mrs Carey reeled off, was glad she'd bought the brochure to refresh her memory.

Then they were led up the wide, sweeping staircase to the first floor and the brocade and canopies of the State Bedroom, where royalty had over the centuries been entertained. The private apartments were cordoned off, but one of the large rooms had been made into a museum of family history, with more portraits and glass cases of medals, decorations and letters from various battle fronts. On display at the far end were the robes worn by the present Duke and Duchess at the Coronation.

The tour ended in the basement, where the huge kitchens, now superseded by more convenient facilities, preserved their open ranges, and meat hooks hung from the ceiling. The dairy next door housed a collection of butter churns, while the laundry, also lovingly restored, retained its pump and an ancient pair of coppers for boiling clothes.

It was with a feeling almost of displacement that they emerged from a side door into the twentieth century. Helen, still caught in the past, followed Melissa and Mrs Carey along the terrace to the glass-fronted Orangery, where small tables were laid for lunch.

'Well, what did you think of it all?' queried Miss Chalmers, seating herself beside Helen and sliding her unused camera under the chair.

'A surfeit of splendour,' Helen said.

'Indeed. And I'm glad to sit down, I can tell you! I find it very tiring, walking slowly and stopping all the time to look at things.'

They were joined at their table by Mr and Mrs Highton, one of the middle-aged couples on the course, and Helen was relieved that Valentine Perry, who'd been making his way towards them, had been forestalled. She was anxious to dispel any idea he might have that, since they'd travelled out here together, they were companions for the day.

Lunch consisted of soup and rolls, quiche with salad and apple pie and cream, all of it either cooked or grown on the premises. During the meal, they discussed what they hoped to see of the grounds during the afternoon.

'Melissa mentioned a murder,' Mrs Highton said, her eyes wide. 'Does anyone know anything about it?'

'The body of a young woman was found in the lily pond,' Miss Chalmers told her. 'Actually, it turned out to be manslaughter, but there was a real murder in the village soon afterwards.'

'Good gracious me!' Mrs Highton's eyes were popping. 'And did they find out who'd committed them?'

'Oh yes, justice was done all round,' Miss Chalmers returned drily. 'Incidentally, I shouldn't mention them in Mrs Carey's hearing; she was involved in both cases.'

They all glanced instinctively at the table where the guide sat talking to Melissa. 'How awful for her!' said Mrs Highton in hushed tones.

'But interesting for everyone else,' Helen commented, adding with a smile, 'We're lucky to have you with us, Miss Chalmers, to bring the history of the house right up to date.'

'Well, I live in the county and take what I like to think is an intelligent interest in local affairs.' The slightly pompous words were offset by a sudden smile. 'In other words, I'm incurably nosy! I devour all the local papers and have a fairly retentive memory. My brother insists I should have been a detective!'

Their conversation was interrupted by Melissa rising to her feet and clapping her hands for attention. 'Ladies and gentlemen, when you've finished your lunch you are free to walk round the grounds. The antique market and gift shop are, I'm afraid, closed at this time of year, but there's still plenty to see, and those of you who bought the brochure will find the grounds mapped out at the back of it. But do please assemble at the coach promptly at four o'clock.'

There was a scraping of chairs and Miss Chalmers retrieved her camera. 'At least I can use it to my heart's content in the grounds,' she said with a smile.

The Hightons had moved away. 'May I walk round with you?' Helen asked. 'You can advise me of the best places to see, though I think I'll give the lily pond a miss.'

'I can't say I blame you. Yes, I'll be glad of your company. The statues in the Italian Garden are well worth a visit.'

The afternoon passed pleasantly. The grounds were vast, but there were rustic benches at strategic points, so it was possible to rest briefly and take in the panoramic views, though too cold to sit still for long. They visited the folly, lost themselves in the maze as was expected of them, marvelled at the topiary and, keeping an eye on the time, gradually wended their way back towards the main gates.

It was as they were walking through longer grass between the trees that Helen, tugging at her scarf to ward off the strengthening wind, inadvertently caught it in her necklace. Before she realized what was happening, the string snapped and a shower of beads went cascading to the ground.

'Oh, *no*!' Helplessly she caught at the broken strand, managing to retain the few remaining beads before, stuffing it in her handbag, she went down on her knees to gather up the rest.

Miss Chalmers went to her assistance, bending stiffly, but the beads had scattered over a surprisingly large area and Helen despaired of finding them all.

'I've been meaning to have them restrung,' she lamented. 'I knew it was getting slack – I shouldn't have worn them.'

'Surely that's all?' Miss Chalmers said, straightening with difficulty and passing her a final handful.

'I should think – no, there's another.' But when Helen retrieved the object which had caught her eye, it was not a bead but a small gold button.

'What have you got there?' Miss Chalmers came over and peered down at Helen's palm. 'That's unusual. I'm sure its owner was annoyed to have lost it.'

Helen stood looking at the button, frowning slightly. It was embossed with an old-fashioned sailing ship and the letters CYC were inscribed round the edge.

'I've a feeling I've seen one like it before, though I can't think where.'

'It's certainly distinctive.' Miss Chalmers paused. 'I don't want to hurry you, but if you've collected all your beads, we should be making our way to the coach.'

'Yes – yes, of course.' Helen slid the button with the rest of the beads into the pocket of her handbag and zipped it shut. But the impression of the little sailing ship lodged tantalizingly at the back of her mind as she boarded the coach for the return journey.

*   *   *

116

The evening was also enjoyable. Rooms had been allocated at Melbray where they could wash and change before dinner, and when they returned to the lounge-hall, it was to find drinks being served and competition forms handed out.

'Dotted round the hall and the lecture room,' Melissa told them, 'are a number of objects. I want you to walk round and identify them, then fill in on your forms what you consider to be the date and value of each object. There's a list of choices for each answer, so all you have to do is tick a, b or c. Then put your name at the top, and hand the forms in before we go to dinner. The results of the competition will be announced over coffee.'

It was the sort of challenge Helen enjoyed and as she walked round, glass in hand, she felt quietly confident of her judgement and impatient to be back in the world of fine art and antiques.

'You're odds-on favourite to win!' teased one of the younger women as she passed, and Helen noted wryly that Valentine Perry was in earshot. She waited for his caustic comment but none came, despite the fact she had managed to avoid his company on the return coach. Perhaps he'd tired of trying to annoy her.

Dinner was duly served, an interesting menu with wine provided, though Helen, remembering her drive home, limited herself to one glass. Too bad this wasn't the normal residential course; then not only would she have been able to enjoy the wine, she'd have been spared the discomfort she now increasingly felt at the Seven Stars. And remembering it for the first time in hours, she experienced the customary twinge of unease. On top of which, she reminded herself, there were Perry's comments about Gordon and the horoscopes still to analyse.

After the meal, as they relaxed over coffee in the lounge-hall, Melissa went through the competition with them, discussing the various objects which they'd had to assess. Helen realized that nearly all her answers had been correct, and she was gratified but not surprised to learn finally that she was the winner. Her prize consisted of a charming little print of Melbray Court in the seventeenth century and a bottle of champagne.

'Now,' Melissa said, when the applause had died away, 'tomorrow, those of you who have friends or relatives in the area may wish to spend the day with them. The rest of us will meet here at ten o'clock and there'll be a coach to take us into Steeple Bayliss. There's a list of church services for those who'd like to attend; the cathedral is magnificent and has a world-famous choir. There are many places of historical interest, and we can arrange a guided walk in the afternoon if enough people are interested.

'If you *won't* be coming with us, please let me know now, so we don't waste time waiting for you.'

Helen, Valentine Perry and Miss Chalmers were the only ones to opt out. 'See you on Monday,' Helen said to the group at large, and, collecting her things, she went out into the cold night to her waiting car.

10

Helen had arranged to call for Penelope at eleven, so for once she was in no hurry. Underlining the relaxed Sunday feeling, the four owners were having their own breakfast in the garden room when she finally appeared. Michael was, as usual, hidden behind his newspaper, but he lowered it to smile at her and ask how her day had gone.

'Very well, thank you. Beckworth House was magnificent.'

'Any sign of the botched break-in?'

'None. It was referred to briefly, but only to explain why cameras couldn't be used in the house.'

'I should have thought those lavish brochures they produce would be more use to thieves than an amateur snapshot.'

Helen smiled her thanks at Stella, who was putting coffee and toast on her table.

'How's your house coming along?' she asked Michael, as Stella moved away.

He picked up his coffee cup and came across to join her. 'No point in shouting at each other,' he commented. 'Actually, I was most annoyed; hardly any work seemed to have been done since I was last there and at this rate, God knows when I'll be able to move in.'

'That's too bad. Did you meet your daughter?'

He made a wry face. 'No, but I didn't really think she'd be free. How about yours?'

'I'm spending today with her.' She paused, then added on impulse, 'Would you like to join us?'

He looked startled. 'That's very kind of you, but mightn't she object?'

'I'm sure she won't. We're only going to wander round Steeple Bayliss, but you'd be very welcome.'

'Well, if you're sure I won't be intruding –'

'Of course not.'

'Then I'd be delighted, provided you let me act as chauffeur and pay for lunch.'

Helen smiled. 'Done!' she said.

If Penelope was surprised to see her mother's escort, she gave no sign of it, merely smiling hello as Helen introduced them.

Yesterday's sunshine had gone, but the day was fine and clear, with high white clouds scudding across the sky before a keen wind. Michael had brought a guide book, and they sat in the car outside the halls of residence studying it.

'Main points of interest appear to be the cathedral, the medieval town hall, and the gorge, which was carved out during the last Ice Age.' He looked up. 'There are some old houses down there, let into the cliff face. Have you seen them?'

The women shook their heads. Helen had previously been to the town only to collect or return her daughter and hadn't stopped to sightsee, while Penelope's knowledge of it after one term was limited to pubs, cinemas and wine bars, with occasional visits to the new shopping mall.

'We must decide where to go for lunch, too,' Michael added. 'I suppose you know the Barley Mow, Penelope? It's always full of students.'

'No, I've never been; we usually go to the Cap and Bells.'

'In that case, let's have lunch there.' He turned to Helen. 'It's a converted grain barge moored on the river. They've preserved its nautical flavour, and there's always something interesting to watch – passing boats, fishermen, swans.'

'It sounds lovely,' Helen said.

'Well, if no one has any strong preferences, I suggest we follow the walk set out in the book. It begins just down the road, at the viaduct.'

The morning passed agreeably, strolling down narrow cobbled streets, peering up at old buildings, watching the ducks on an unexpected pond. They passed the cathedral, immense in its Gothic splendour, but since a service was in progress, postponed their visit until the afternoon.

Michael proved quietly knowledgeable on history and architecture, which added to Helen's enjoyment, and, having explored the town on previous occasions, was able to lead them into unexpected corners – an ancient flight of stone steps, two houses meeting across the street – which they might otherwise have missed.

Their leisurely itinerary brought them finally to the steep road leading down to the river, far beneath the high, wide arches of the viaduct which formed the main entrance to the town. Here, as Michael had told them, was a fascinating collection of houses built into the cliff face, some old, some new, but all harmonizing with their golden-yellow stone-work.

At the river edge a series of small boats bobbed gently on the water, and on the opposite bank were the trees and steep grassy banks of the university grounds.

Ahead lay the grain barge which was their lunch-time objective, and as they approached it the path broadened into a wider, cobbled area with wooden benches and tables where, on warmer days, customers could sit to watch the passing river traffic. Today, the wind skimmed round them, and Helen was glad of the warmth which came to meet them as they went up the gangplank and down the wide, polished staircase into what had once been the hold.

As Michael had said, the conversion was imaginative. Opposite the entrance, a lifebelt painted with the name 'Barley Mow' hung in pride of place, with port and starboard lights on either side, and the walls were decorated with prints of barges and steamboats. Along one of them stretched a polished bar with stools in front of it – most of them occupied – and against another, tables were placed beside small round portholes.

Helen and Pen seated themselves at one while Michael procured a menu from the bar. To Helen's relief, although there were several groups of students dotted about, there were also quite a few people of her own age, including a couple of family parties.

121

During their brief moment alone, Penelope whispered, 'Have you told Dad about this dishy admirer of yours?'

'Don't be ridiculous,' Helen said sharply. 'He's nothing of the kind.'

'Come on, Mum, who are you fooling? He's jolly attentive, and you know it.'

'Only because he's our escort for the day.'

There was no time for more; Michael returned with the menu and their drinks and Helen, aware of her daughter's interested gaze, avoided his eye. But though throughout the meal conversation was continuous, a seed had been sown, and, under cover of her chat, Helen warily examined it.

It was only natural she and Michael should come together, she told herself, since over the weekend they were the sole guests at the Seven Stars. There was no more to it than that. Perhaps he *was* attentive – certainly more than Andrew had been for years – but he was also lonely, which was why she'd invited him along.

And Pen was right, she acknowledged less readily, he was attractive, too, especially when he smiled and his face became less severe. But what of it? Was she supposed only to speak to uninteresting men?

She looked up defiantly, catching Penelope's eye, which closed in a knowing wink. Helen smiled, as much at herself as her daughter, and shook herself free of her introspection.

When they emerged from the barge, the temperature was noticeably cooler and the wind had sharpened. They walked briskly up the hill, the muscles tugging at the backs of their legs, and on reaching the top level, retraced their steps towards the cathedral. But as they approached the close a man came hurrying round the corner, almost bumping into them, and to her astonishment Helen saw that it was Andrew.

He seemed as startled as she was, and it was Penelope who found her voice first. 'Daddy! What on earth are you doing here?'

Andrew bent to kiss her cheek and, after a moment, Helen's. 'Business, what else?'

122

'On a *Sunday*? Why didn't you let us know you were coming?'

'Because it really is business, Pen, and I didn't think there'd be time to see you.'

'You could have phoned Mummy, on the off chance.'

'I haven't got her number.'

'You didn't mention coming when I spoke to you on Wednesday,' Helen reminded him.

'It hadn't been fixed then.'

She wasn't sure she believed him. Perhaps that was why he'd inquired if she'd be home for the weekend – because he himself wouldn't be.

Andrew's eyes had gone questioningly to Michael, silent at their side.

'I'm so sorry,' Helen apologized. 'Andrew, this is Michael Saxton, my fellow lodger. My husband, Michael.'

The two men shook hands in silence, and as they moved apart Andrew's eyes went from Michael's face to a point beyond his shoulder. Helen saw him stiffen and give a minute shake of his head. She turned swiftly. A woman who had been hurrying towards them halted abruptly, hesitated, then crossed the road and walked quickly round the opposite corner.

Andrew met and held Helen's gaze, and when she made no comment, said, 'I thought the course extended over the weekend?'

'It does, but today's schedule was optional, so I'm spending it with Pen.'

There was a brief, uncomfortable silence. Then Penelope said, 'Well, can you join us now? We're going to look round the cathedral.'

'I can't, love, honestly. I'm meeting a colleague; we have an appointment at three o'clock. I really am sorry about this, but I'll be up again soon, I promise, and we'll have a slap-up meal. Am I forgiven?'

'I suppose so.'

Andrew turned to Helen. 'See you on Saturday, then.'

She nodded, and with a quick smile which embraced them all, he hurried away. Helen did not look after him, knowing beyond doubt that he would turn down the road the woman had taken. *Was* she a colleague, or something more? That Andrew might have someone else had never occurred to her, but before she could examine the possibility, Michael said rallyingly, 'Well, are we still going to the cathedral?'

She pulled herself together, pushing the oddly disconcerting little episode out of her mind.

'Most certainly,' she said.

But the meeting with Andrew left a shadow over the day, and the spontaneity had gone out of it. They walked dutifully round the vast building, looking at tombs of martyrs and saints, at marble effigies and gilded eagles, at cherubs and satyrs and vivid, medieval stained glass. But there was a constraint between them which the occasional laboured comment did nothing to dispel, and Helen wasn't surprised, when they emerged at last into the grey afternoon, that Penelope suggested they drop her off to prepare for the next day's lectures.

She made no effort to dissuade her, wondering whether Pen too had seen the woman who so abruptly changed course, or whether the change in Helen's own mood had affected her. Whatever the reason, the afternoon was past saving.

They returned to the car park near the viaduct where they'd begun their walk and drove the short distance to the university. Helen kissed her daughter.

'If you've an evening free this week, perhaps we could have dinner?' It was a veiled apology and Penelope gave her a quick smile. 'That'd be great, Mum. Goodbye, Michael. Thanks for lunch.' She climbed out of the car, turned to wave, and disappeared – thankfully, Helen didn't doubt – into the halls of residence.

'I think a cup of tea is indicated, with perhaps a toasted teacake?'

She forced a smile. 'Good idea, if anywhere's open on a Sunday.'

'The hotels will be.'

They drove back over the viaduct to the White Swan

124

where, Helen remembered, Sir Clifford Rudge stayed on his visits to Melbray. It was an old-fashioned hotel with a hushed, Sunday-afternoon feel about it, and they went into the lounge and took a window seat overlooking the river. Afternoon tea was in progress and there was the comforting smell of buttered toast and the clink of china.

Helen declined the offer of sandwiches or pastries, reiterating Michael's suggestion of toasted teacakes. When the waiter had moved away, he said quietly, 'That was unfortunate.'

'What was?'

'Meeting your husband like that.'

'How do you mean?'

'Come on, Helen, you know quite well what I mean.' He paused. 'Didn't he know you were up here? He seemed surprised to see you.'

'I'd told him we were working over the weekend. He wouldn't have expected me to be in town.'

But that wasn't the point; the meeting had patently not been that of a happily married couple. The fact hadn't escaped Michael, and might also account for Penelope's subdued spirits.

'But if he hadn't your phone number –'

'I didn't give it to him,' she admitted after a moment, 'because I – needed a bit of space.'

'Yet you rang him.'

'Yes. That evening I was –' But how could she explain the unease which, increasing all week, had been accentuated by the phone-call during dinner and Terry Pike's interrogation afterwards? For Michael was himself part of that scenario, and had compounded her anxiety with his comment that the hit-and-run might not be an accident.

'You were what?' he prompted, when she didn't continue. Unable to explain, she simply shook her head. He laid a hand over hers.

'Helen, I don't want to pry, but if it would help to talk, I've been there myself.'

She gave in suddenly, needing to talk about it.

'Did you see that woman?'

'Yes.'

'She was with him.'

'Yes.'

'Why didn't he want us to meet her?' For *us*, read *me*, she thought bitterly.

'There could be a number of reasons. If she's his colleague –'

'*If*?'

'– she might be trying to keep a low profile.'

'But he's not in MI5, for God's sake! I've met his colleagues before.'

'Women?'

She thought back. 'Not that I remember, but there are plenty in the firm.'

There was a silence while they both thought of one in particular. She'd been quite young – mid-thirties, probably – and her brisk stride had given an impression of determination. She'd worn a loose tweed coat with the collar turned up and her hair was short, curly, and chestnut-brown. Remembering, Helen was surprised she had taken in so much in that fleeting glimpse.

The waiter returned and began to unload his tray. The teacakes were crisp and golden, glistening with butter. Michael waited till he moved away. Then, as Helen poured the tea, he said quietly, 'You're wondering if there's something between them?'

Her eyes flew to his face and he said quickly, 'I'm sorry, I'd no right –'

She gave a little shake of her head. 'From the way he behaved, it's a possibility.'

'But only a possibility. He might be having the same doubts about us.'

Remembering Penelope's comments, Helen's cheeks burned; but she said lightly, 'In less than a week?'

'It has been known.' He paused, then added gently, 'But the mere fact that you're wondering shows there's something wrong. Was that why you came on the course?'

'Partly, but also because I genuinely want to get back to working with antiques.' She reached for a teacake, not looking at him. 'You're right, though; things have been strained for a while.' It seemed disloyal to talk about it, but her emotions were now so mixed up it was a relief to voice at least some of them. She almost hoped Michael would probe further, but instead he said, 'If he's working on the Stately Home break-ins, he must have a lead in this area.'

'Not necessarily; he's on several other cases, too.' She gave a wry smile. 'And whether or not that woman is his mistress, it would have been a genuine business meeting. This is the last place he'd choose for an illicit weekend, with both Pen and me in the vicinity.'

She looked at Michael's reflective face and, since they were discussing personal matters, asked curiously, 'What went wrong with your marriage?'

He shrugged. 'Incompatibility. Sounds like legal jargon, but it's the best way I can describe it. We got to the stage when everything we did either hurt or irritated the other. God knows how we stuck it so long, but as soon as the children were self-reliant we parted, with much relief on both sides.'

'Our children are self-reliant, too.'

'It's not an obligatory time to separate,' Michael said with a smile. 'Look, you're having a brief spell apart to take stock, right?'

She nodded.

'Then the meeting was no bad thing. His suspicions, if any, are unfounded. Yours might be, too, but at least it's jolted you both, forced you to consider how you feel.'

Outside the window a soft, steady rain had started to fall, drawing a gauze curtain over the river below. Undeterred, a line of swans swam majestically downstream and Helen watched their progress, her thoughts still chaotic. Even if the woman were no more than a colleague, the pretence of normality she'd maintained over Christmas had been exposed as a sham. Her next meeting with her daughter would not be easy.

Quite suddenly, she needed to be alone, to come to terms with such facts as had presented themselves. She said abruptly, 'Can we go now?'

If Michael was surprised by her mood swing, he made no comment, simply called for the bill and led her out of the over-stuffy room into the rain-chilled afternoon. They hurried to the car, waited till the windscreen wipers had cleared a space to see through, and drove up on to the main road.

After several minutes, Michael said wryly, 'I hope you're not regretting having invited me to join you.'

'Of course not, we were glad of your company.' She was careful to include Penelope in that gladness. 'And your comments added a lot to the sightseeing – about the old window tax, for instance, which I'd forgotten.'

They swung off the road at the Seven Stars and had to negotiate a car parked in front of the house.

'It's Dominic's,' Michael said resignedly. 'He always parks there – too bone idle to go round the back like everyone else.'

Helen hoped she wouldn't be challenged to another sparring match. At the moment she felt incapable of holding her own, but perhaps after some time to herself, she'd be better company.

'Thanks for lunch,' she said as they hurried inside out of the rain. 'See you later.' And she went up the stairs to her room.

Webb sat in his favourite armchair, a mug of tea cooling rapidly at his side. Dammit, there must be *something* they could do. Over a million's worth of art and antiques nicked, a peer of the realm murdered, and still, though large portions of the country's police forces were working flat out, barely a clue with which to start hunting the perpetrators.

So what *had* they got? Ten country house burglaries over two years, the last couple, Plaistead and Buckhurst, only two weeks apart. And there was the foiled attempt at Beckworth, which would have made three in as many weeks.

That was on the debit side. On the plus, all they had were a few microscopic hairs, and tyre marks of a vehicle allegedly parked near the scene. Big deal. Not unnaturally, the vague description offered by the couple who'd seen the car had been little help.

Since there'd not been so much as a sniff of the stolen goods, it seemed likely that the jewellery at least had been broken up and reset, possibly on the continent. But what of the other, equally identifiable, items – miniatures, porcelain, clocks, silver – all of which had disappeared without trace? Had the transactions taken place immediately, before the authorities could be put on their guard?

The other possibility, that the thieves were stealing to order for specific buyers, was even more worrying, since such a set-up was almost impossible to penetrate.

He leant back and stared at the ceiling, mentally running through the articles stolen and experiencing the usual stab of frustration at the inconsistency in their value. When the pride of the collection was taken, that was at least understandable. It was the other times, when the theft was of little more than a trinket, that really irked him.

What game were the thieves playing, and for what stakes? Why lay themselves open to such risks for items of little consequence? True, in themselves they were charming enough – Lady Cleverley's statuette, a Victorian mourning ring, a couple of snuff-boxes. It was the fact that they were surrounded by priceless pieces, which the thieves ignored, that was incomprehensible. Why, in God's name, take the incalculable risk of neutralizing alarms and forcing entry, then not ensure that such a gamble was worthwhile?

Grimly, Webb hoped that when they finally did catch up with them, it would be on one such frivolous errand.

Then there was the Randall Tovey theft, which Hannah had mentioned again the other evening. Another case of searching for needles in haystacks, and pretty sensitive needles, at that. The threatened arrest of the Chief Constable's wife still sent shivers down his back, though John Baker had been within his rights. Yet again he went through the possible suspects: Lady Soames, the duchess and her daughter, and some five dozen of the wealthiest and most influential women in the country.

It had been hard to explain to Hannah, understandably concerned for her friend's reputation, that they couldn't afford the manpower necessary to fingerprint such a large number for a ten-thousand-pound ring. Which consideration, he'd been careful to stress, would have applied equally had the people concerned been considerably less illustrious than in fact they were.

All the police could do was hope local jewellers would keep their eyes open for any ring reported to have been 'found by my little girl in the street'.

He sighed deeply. The year had not started well. He could only hope it would improve.

11

When Helen came down for dinner, Dominic was propped, as before, in front of the bar talking to Gordon, but there was no sign of Caroline. Since it seemed impolite to go and sit by the fire, as she'd have preferred, she tentatively approached them, conscious that they immediately broke off their conversation.

'Good evening, Helen,' Gordon said with false heartiness. 'And what can I get you?'

'A sherry, please.'

Dominic glanced at her with a silent nod. His previous lightheartedness seemed to have deserted him and his face looked drawn.

Gordon slid her glass across to her. 'Had a good day?'

'Yes, thanks. We were exploring Steeple Bayliss. I'd no idea it was so old.' She paused, then turned to Dominic. 'Is Caroline with you?'

'No, she stayed with her father. He's not expected to last the night.'

No wonder he was looking concerned. 'I'm so sorry,' she said awkwardly. 'What a difficult time for you all.'

'Will she stay on when you go back to London?' Gordon asked.

'I imagine so. Even if Roderick's still with us in the morning, he hasn't long to go, and she'd only have to turn round and come straight back.' He finished his drink. 'Intimations of mortality are not my scene, I'm afraid. My instinct is to cut and run at the first sign of approaching demise.'

Stella had joined them in time to hear his last comments. 'How's Caro bearing up?' she inquired.

'Not well. She's very jittery and liable to burst into tears at any moment.'

'Poor girl,' Helen said softly. 'I remember how I felt when my father died.'

It seemed the cheerful evening which she'd hoped would dispel her own problems was not forthcoming. Michael and Nicholas joined them, and after another drink all round – which Helen felt in need of – they went in to dinner.

The atmosphere continued sombre, despite the excellent fare that Kate had prepared, and it was left to Michael to keep the conversational ball rolling, with Helen making sporadic attempts to help him.

It was as the main course was being served that, glancing at Dominic opposite her, she noticed the gold buttons on his blazer. In the subdued light and at a distance of three feet it was difficult to make out the design, but they were certainly embossed and she was almost sure it was with an old-fashioned sailing boat.

She said casually, 'Those are very splendid buttons, Dominic. Is that a ship on them?'

He nodded.

'What does CYC stand for?'

'Talk about 20/20 vision!' Nicholas exclaimed with a laugh. 'I couldn't have made that out across the table.'

Helen kept her eyes inquiringly on Dominic.

'Chardsey Yacht Club,' he replied.

'Where's that?'

'In Surrey, where my parents live.'

She took the plate that was handed to her and helped herself to vegetables, her mind racing. As far as she could see, none of his buttons was missing, though he could have replaced it. Should she say she'd found an identical one? Something held her back and she decided to wait awhile and approach the subject from a different angle.

The meal continued, with Michael regaling them about the day in Steeple Bayliss and lunch at the Barley Mow. He did not, to Helen's relief, mention having met Andrew. The others nodded and smiled in appropriate places, making little contribution.

During the dessert, Helen, helping Michael out but also putting her plan into effect, said brightly, 'And yesterday I went to Beckworth House. Have you been there, Dominic?'

He looked surprised at again being singled out. 'No, I can't say I have.'

'It's well worth seeing. I'm sure you'd enjoy it.'

He shook his head. 'I've never been one for stately home visiting. With all due respect, the thought of traipsing slowly along a drugget with a crowd of gawping tourists fills me with horror.'

Helen joined in the general laughter and let the subject drop, but her mind still circled round the button. It must have been lost fairly recently, since it was too shiny to have lain there since the end of last season. But the house was not yet open to the public and no one in their group had had such buttons. Perhaps another private party had been there, but it was certainly a coincidence if it had included someone from the same yacht club as Dominic.

The meal ended, and he declined the offer of a brandy.

'I think I should be getting back,' he said, and they all moved into the hall.

Stella hovered anxiously. 'Our love to Caro. Tell her we're thinking of her.'

Dominic nodded and, gripping the sleeves of his blazer to stop them riding up, let Gordon help him on with his raincoat. But not before Helen, with a queer little jerk of her heart, had seen the empty space on one sleeve where a second gold button should have been.

She did not sleep well that night. The mystery of the button, the meeting with Andrew, even Pen's comments about Michael being her admirer, circled endlessly in her brain, making her restless and wide awake.

Was Andrew having an affair with that woman? Was that why he'd stopped her approaching them? What was he doing in Steeple Bayliss anyway? Should she tackle him about it when she got home? She'd been hoping her homecoming would be a time of reconciliation, not renewed hostilities, but their marriage stood no chance until these questions had been answered.

Her overactive brain veered to another problem. Why had Dominic lied about visiting Beckworth? There was little doubt that he had; coincidence couldn't be stretched indefinitely and the remaining button on his cuff exactly matched the one she had found, even to being slightly smaller than those on the front.

So *when* had he been there? Recently, certainly. Yet if he so disliked visiting stately homes, he was unlikely to have joined a private party for that purpose. Perhaps he knew the Hampshires? But if so, why deny having visited them?

There could be only one reason for the lie; he did not want anyone to know he'd been there. Again, why?

A voice in Helen's head stated flatly, *There was an attempted break-in at Beckworth on Monday, and the would-be thieves escaped across the grounds.*

A wave of heat washed over her and she immediately dismissed the idea. *Dominic* a thief? Whatever reason could he have, with his apartment at St Katharine's Dock and his highly paid job in the City?

Then an even more preposterous thought encroached. *If* he was involved in the Stately Home burglaries, was he also responsible for Lord Cleverley's murder?

She sat up abruptly, swung her legs out of bed and paced agitatedly about the room. If this fantastic scenario were true, did the Cains and Warrens know of Dominic's activities? Did Terry? Did Michael? And what of the horoscope column — how did that fit into the puzzle?

She stood in the middle of the cold room, her hands to her head. All at once the little niggling queries that had worried her had swelled into one great, overriding question mark, and one which she could no longer keep to herself. She dared not confide in Michael, nor, in the present circumstances, could she approach Andrew, even if she knew where he was. There was only one course open to her: she must go to the police.

The seriousness of the step appalled her. Would they, like

Pen, think she was overreacting? But even if they did, at least she'd have handed over responsibility.

The decision reached, Helen took a deep, steadying breath. Then, suddenly aware of the cold night air on her sweating body, she climbed back into bed and determinedly closed her eyes.

Helen was heavy-eyed the next morning and it took an effort to dress, go down to breakfast and behave as though nothing were wrong.

But it was quite possible nothing was. The lucidity with which she had viewed the situation in the night had dissipated, leaving her muddled and confused as though it had all been a bad dream. She even began to wonder whether she would, after all, go to the police. She'd simply make a fool of herself, pouring out half-baked suspicions like a neurotic middle-aged housewife.

Warily she watched them under lowered lids – Stella, pale but composed with her coffeepot, Michael behind his newspaper. It was a normal Monday morning, she told herself; everyone was preparing for the start of the week. Michael would go to his office and Terry Pike would be on his way back from Blackpool. She thought of his searching eyes and the persistence of his questioning about Andrew and his work. Why was he so interested? Was he working with Dominic?

Her eyes followed Stella as she moved about the room. Dominic was a family friend; surely the four of them must know what he was up to?

If, Helen reminded herself carefully, he was up to anything.

'Helen?'

She started and turned to Michael.

'I said, are you all right? You look a bit under the weather this morning.'

'I didn't sleep too well,' she admitted.

He nodded gravely, no doubt thinking she'd been fretting about Andrew. As, in part, she had.

'Remember I'm here, if you want to talk about it.'

'Thanks.' She pushed away her uneaten roll and stood up.

'What are you tackling today?'

She stiffened, then realized he was referring to the course. 'English watercolours in the eighteenth and nineteenth centuries.'

He smiled. 'That should keep you busy. You'll be back for dinner?'

'Yes.'

What would have happened by dinner-time? She had decided to attend all the day's lectures, since to miss one would cause comment, and to drive into Steeple Bayliss at the end of the afternoon. No doubt someone would direct her to the police station – if her nerve had not failed by then.

Michael pushed back his chair and accompanied her out to the car, waiting while she unlocked it.

'You're sure you're all right to drive?'

She forced a smile. 'Of course I am!'

'You look decidedly shaky to me. Take care, then.' And he bent and kissed her cheek.

Hardly knowing what she was doing, Helen clambered inside, her hands fumbling at the controls. The engine started with a surprised whoosh, the wheels spurted gravel and the car shot forward. Frantically she spun the wheel just in time to make the turning into the narrow passageway leading to the road. A supreme example of how not to drive, she thought, furious with herself. It would have convinced Michael she was in no fit state – unless he attributed her performance to his kiss.

Cheeks flaming, she put her foot down hard on the accelerator and sped towards Melbray.

Somehow, the day crawled by. At one point, Rose Chalmers startled her by saying suddenly, 'Did you remember where you'd seen that button?'

'I – yes, on someone I met at the digs.'

'I'm sure he was glad to have it back.'

Helen smiled and made no reply. Would he have been? What would have happened if, at the dinner-table, she had unzipped her purse and handed Dominic the button she'd

136

found? He could hardly have denied it was his, with the space on his cuff. Would she have met with an 'accident', like Molly?

She shuddered and, at Miss Chalmers's raised eyebrows, gave an embarrassed little laugh. 'Someone walking over my grave!' she said, and immediately wished she hadn't.

Valentine Perry joined her again at lunch. 'Did you compare notes on Beckworth with your hosts?' he asked her.

'I told them about the visit, if that's what you mean.'

'Cain did a feature on it last year. I remember him saying he'd lugged the whole family along with him.'

Her flicker of interest died. Neither Gordon nor Nicholas belonged to Chardsey Yacht Club.

The hour between three-thirty and four-thirty was the longest she could remember. Countless times, despite the interesting lecture, her eyes wandered to the grandfather clock that ticked the day away. Once or twice she was sure it had stopped, but four-thirty came at last and Helen, excusing herself from the usual questions and chat, hurried out to her car. There was a heavy weight in her stomach and she felt slightly sick at the prospect ahead of her. Suppose she was entirely wrong? Could she be charged with false accusation? Would her comments be treated as confidential?

On the outskirts of Steeple Bayliss she drew into a garage, filled up with petrol, and as casually as possible asked where the police station was.

'Maybury Street, duck,' the mechanic told her cheerfully. 'Turn left off the High Street opposite the Pickwick, then right at the T-junction and the nick's on your right.'

She knew the Pickwick wine bar; she and Pen had lunched there. Helen thanked him and returned to the car. The rush-hour traffic was starting, but most of it was in the opposite direction and did not delay her until she reached the High Street, which was congested with traffic. With two solid lines of cars, it was as well she did not need to make a right turn. Following the directions she'd been given, she found the police station without difficulty, halfway along Maybury Street.

Even then, if there'd been nowhere to park she might have

driven past it and gone home; but fate didn't let her off so easily. As she approached, a motorist drew away from a parking meter and Helen slid into his place. The die was cast. She dropped coins in the meter, crossed the road and went up the steps to the swing doors.

The foyer was warmed by large radiators along the wall. Several people were milling aimlessly about, among them a woman with a crying child. As Helen passed, she was saying soothingly, 'Someone'll hand him in, pet, don't you worry.'

A uniformed sergeant was making notes at a desk and Helen went over to him. He looked up. 'Yes, love?'

'I want to speak to someone in authority,' she said, feeling foolish.

He raised an eyebrow. 'We're all in authority, in a manner of speaking.'

'It's –' She seized on something he would know about. 'It's to do with the hit-and-run the other week.'

'Well, that was a CID matter. Perhaps Sergeant Hopkins could help you.'

As he was speaking, a handsome, fair-haired man who was passing stopped and came over to them.

He smiled at Helen, seeming to sense her nervousness. 'Perhaps I can help? I'm DI Ledbetter and I've been dealing with the hit-and-run.'

She said gratefully, 'Then I'd very much like to talk to you.'

He nodded. 'Send some tea in to Interview Room 2, will you, Bob?' He glanced at Helen. 'Milk and sugar?'

'Just milk, please.'

He guided her across the tiled floor to a small room, followed her inside and closed the door.

'Now, Mrs –'

'Campbell.'

'– Mrs Campbell, if you'd like to sit down, you can tell me all about it. Have you any objection if I switch on the tape? I've no writing equipment with me and it saves having to remember.'

'None at all.' But she was aware that her voice had become stilted.

'Just try to forget about it,' he advised. 'The time is sixteen-fifty, I've told you I'm DI Ledbetter, so if you'll just give me your address we can get on with it.'

Helen did so, and he looked up in surprise. 'You're a long way from home.'

'I'm attending a course at Melbray, and staying at the Seven Stars.'

'Ah yes, the girl worked there, didn't she?'

There was a tap on the door and a policewoman came in with a tray and two polystyrene mugs.

'Not quite the Ritz, I'm afraid,' Ledbetter said with a grin. 'Right, Mrs Campbell, what's troubling you?'

She hesitated, then said in a rush, 'You'll probably think I'm mad, Inspector, but quite a lot of things are.'

'You mentioned the hit-and-run?'

'Yes. I was there that evening, at the Seven Stars. I'd brought my daughter back to university and got caught in the fog, so I spent the night there.' Her hands tightened on her lap.

'I drove round to the back, following the sign to the car park, and drew up at the far end by the other cars. But before I could get out, a girl came running out of the house, followed by a man shouting at her to come back. She didn't, and after a minute he went back inside and slammed the door.'

'Go on.'

'Well, I didn't think any more of it then. But later, when I came down to dinner, I overheard someone say, "I thought she'd gone. God knows how much she heard." '

'And you thought he was referring to the girl?'

'I didn't really think anything, except that I hoped he wouldn't think *I* was eavesdropping and I moved quickly away.'

'Who was speaking, Mrs Campbell?'

She gave a little shrug. 'It's funny, but I hadn't met any of them then, and since I have, I've found it hard to reproduce the voice in my head.'

'So you're not sure?'

'I'm afraid not.'

'Was it the same man that ran after the girl?'

'I assumed so at the time.' She paused. 'Yes, I think it was. Anyway, later a young man came knocking on the door saying there'd been an accident, but of course I didn't connect it with Molly, who'd left much earlier. That's all that happened then, except that I read about the Melbray course in the local paper. A week or so later I decided to apply for it, and since it wasn't residential, booked in again at the Seven Stars. And it was on my return, last Sunday, that I heard Molly'd been killed.'

There was a brief silence. Then Ledbetter said, 'And you're wondering if it was deliberate?'

She nodded, sipping her tea and not looking at him.

'Well, I can set your mind at rest on that score, at least. We found the hit-and-run driver; he's a seventeen-year-old youth who was out joy-riding. So whatever Molly heard or didn't hear, you can rest assured she wasn't killed because of it. Her death was an accident.'

Helen drew a long breath. 'Then perhaps it's not worth bothering you with the other things. They've probably got an equally rational explanation.'

'You're not bothering me, Mrs Campbell. It was public-spirited of you to come along, though if I may say so, you took your time about it.'

'I thought I was just being neurotic. But when things began to build up –'

'What things?'

'This sounds ludicrous, I know, but do you see the horoscope column in the *Evening News*?'

'My wife does.'

Stumblingly, Helen told him of Cain's connection with it, about the repetitions that came under 'Tomorrow's Birthday', the tension with which her comment had been received, and finally Valentine Perry's remarks about the changes made to the forecast.

'As he said, it's not as though it's anything important, but the point is the added sentences are always similar: "Someone is waiting to hear from you" or "A friend would like to hear from you". Do you see what I mean? As though it's asking someone to get in touch.' She gave a little laugh. 'It sounds like something out of Bulldog Drummond, doesn't it?'

'Have you any idea who this message, if it is one, is intended for?'

'None, nor how any reply's received. It's probably nothing at all, and I'm just wasting your time. In fact, if it hadn't been for what happened at the weekend I should never have come here.'

'And what happened at the weekend?'

She told him of her visit to Beckworth House, of finding the button, and noticing Dominic had one missing after he denied having been there. And suddenly the inspector's interest was more than mere politeness.

'Have you got this button with you?'

She opened her purse and handed it over. Ledbetter studied it in his palm. Helen said, 'The letters stand for Chardsey Yacht Club. I asked him. It's in Surrey.'

'Who exactly is Dominic Hardy, Mrs Campbell?'

'A friend of the family, who was at school with Nicholas Warren. Michael Saxton, who's been at the Seven Stars for some months, says he comes quite often. He has an apartment at St Katharine's Dock.'

'Why does he keep coming here?'

'Because his girlfriend's parents live nearby and her father's dying.'

'What's the girlfriend's name?'

'Caroline. I must have heard her surname, but I can't — oh yes, I think it's Budd.'

'Do you know where her parents live? Or their initials?'

'Not their address, but Dominic spoke of her father as Roderick.'

Abruptly he changed the subject. 'You wouldn't know what car Hardy drives?'

'A blue Saab nine thousand,' she answered promptly. 'My brother has one, so I recognized it.'

Ledbetter leant forward, his eyes gleaming. 'Now that *is* helpful. Where does he park it?' Please God, not where half a dozen cars had been since.

'At the front of the house, almost blocking access to the rear. Michael says he always parks there.'

'Mrs Campbell, you're a wonder!'

'You think he's tied in with the Stately Homes?'

'We'll be taking a good look at him.' He paused. 'I'm sure I needn't ask you to say nothing of your visit here.'

She gave a little shiver. 'No.'

'Do you know where Hardy is now?'

'I think he was going back to London, but Caro's staying on because her father hasn't much longer to live.'

'I want you to think carefully. Has anything else happened at the Seven Stars which struck you as strange, even if it seemed unimportant?'

'Well, Terry Pike, who's also been there a while, was very interested to hear my husband's a loss adjuster working on some of the Stately Homes claims.'

Ledbetter raised an eyebrow. 'That interests me, too. We might have spoken on the phone.'

'Oh? I suppose you wouldn't know why he was up here yesterday?' Was it really only yesterday? It already seemed days ago.

'I'm afraid I've no idea. Didn't he tell you?'

'He just said he was on business.'

If the inspector thought it strange a wife should ask someone else what her husband was doing, he made no comment.

'Do you know what Mr Pike's job is?' he asked instead.

'No, only that he commutes from Blackpool and goes home at weekends.'

The inspector drummed his fingers thoughtfully, then looked up at her. 'Anything else? Anything at all?'

'Well, there was the phone-call, but –'

'What phone-call?'

'It was on Wednesday, while we were at dinner. The phone started to ring and everybody froze and then, with one accord, looked at their watches. So I did, too, and it was exactly eight o'clock. Nicholas went to answer it, and Gordon said it wasn't worth putting his dinner in the oven because he wouldn't be long, and I wondered how he knew. But he was right, and when Nicholas came back, he never said who

142

was on the phone and no one asked him. It didn't seem natural, somehow.'

'It didn't strike you it might have been in answer to the horoscope?'

She stared at him, a pulse beating in her throat. 'Are you serious?'

'Not really, just thinking aloud. What day was it you saw the bit about someone waiting for a call?'

Helen thought back. 'Monday, I think. But if they're in telephone contact, why didn't they ring themselves in the first place instead of all the rigmarole with the horoscopes?'

'I've no idea. Of course, the phone-call might have nothing to do with the horoscopes, and the horoscopes themselves might be entirely innocuous.'

He leant back in his chair and surveyed her. 'It has been a very interesting half-hour, Mrs Campbell. Thank you for coming to see us.'

'What happens now?' Helen asked, aware she was being politely dismissed.

His mouth lifted humorously. 'We shall continue with our inquiries. But do please be discreet. It's better that no one should suspect you've been here.'

He showed her out to the foyer, watched her manipulate the swing doors, then, pressing the security buttons, went upstairs to his office, where he perched on the edge of his desk and picked up the phone.

The first call was to his superior officer, with whom he spoke at some length. The second was briefer and more succinct.

'I need two addresses urgently: that of Roderick Budd, which will be somewhere local, and Dominic Hardy, in the St Katharine's Dock area of London.' After a minute or two the voice came back to him, and he made a note on his pad. Then he dialled a third time, and a voice said in his ear, 'Webb.'

'Dave, there have been developments and I need to be in several places at once. Trouble is, we're short of manpower, what with a flu epidemic and a major road accident this afternoon. Any chance of your helping out? If you need an incentive, it's a lead on the Stately Homes caper.'

Webb's voice quickened with interest. 'I'm sure I can clear it. What's happened?'

Speaking rapidly, Ledbetter outlined his suspicions about Dominic Hardy and his girlfriend. 'We'll have to move fast, before they can warn each other we're on their track. Trouble is, Hardy's back in London now and will have to be collected. His girlfriend's still in SB, though, so if you could pick her up –'

'Look, Chris, why don't I go to London? It makes more sense for you to stay on the spot if you've several irons in the fire.'

'Are you sure you don't mind? Thanks, Dave – I owe you one. As soon as you've got him, give me a bell on my mobile. I'll have SOCO standing by to hot-foot it to the Seven Stars and, with luck, lift his tyre prints.'

'The guesthouse, you mean? You reckon they'd tip him off?'

'I don't know what I reckon about that lot at the moment. There's all sorts of baloney about horoscopes and God knows what, but the first priority is to get Hardy and Budd here for questioning.'

'Right. So what are we bringing them in for?'

'Suspicion of burglary will do for now. Good luck, Dave, and thanks again.'

Ledbetter put down the phone, stood up and stretched. Things were moving at last.

12

Helen drove back to the Seven Stars with her mind churning. She realized now that she hadn't expected the police to take her seriously – had, in fact, been hoping that they wouldn't. She'd imagined herself recounting the whole business to Andrew, and both of them laughing over her preposterous suspicions.

But the production of the button had changed everything. From polite interest, speculation and reassurance, the inspector had snapped to attention, and, having elicited all the information she had to offer, been quick to dispatch her. Obviously there were more important things to do than talk to her any longer.

He'd been very interested in Dominic's car, she remembered – even as to where it was parked. Would he send someone out to the Seven Stars? If so, would anyone there guess she'd been the one to lay information? And suppose Michael were involved?

She had a surreal picture in her mind of them all being led out in handcuffs to waiting police cars – the Cains, the Warrens, Terry and Michael, and she, the only one left in the house, watching from a window.

The detective hadn't been convinced by the horoscopes, though, and the more she thought about it, the more outrageous her hypothesis seemed. As she'd said herself, why weren't the messages – if messages they were – relayed by phone?

Nevertheless, when she let herself into the house to find the hall deserted she went quickly to the paper on the table, her hands trembling as she searched for the column and 'Tomorrow's Birthday'.

And there it was. *If you contact a friend, you might learn something to your advantage.*

Would the inspector, busy 'continuing his inquiries', as he put it, think to look at the column when he arrived home tonight? And be struck by the similarity of the phrasing?

Refolding the paper and dropping it back on the table, she wondered if there were any way she could check with Valentine Perry that the last sentence had been an addition. And if so, when it had been inserted.

She went to her room and forced herself to sit down in the red chair and read her book till it was time to wash and change for dinner.

She must be completely natural, she told herself as she went downstairs, giving no inkling that she half-suspected them of nefarious doings. And, looking round the table at the now-familiar faces, it was in any case impossible to believe.

Then, just as she was allowing herself to relax, Terry leant back in his chair and glanced sideways at her. 'And what, might I ask, were you doing down at the nick today, Helen?'

She jumped, swivelling to face him, and he gave a short laugh. 'Look at that – guilt written all over her! What's your dark secret, then? Been arrested for shoplifting?'

She was aware of stillness round the table, of six pairs of eyes fastened on her face, above all of the inspector's warning: *It's better that no one should suspect you've been here.*

Then Michael said, 'Was it about your necklace?'

She flung him a look of profound gratitude. 'Yes – yes, I –'

Michael continued smoothly, 'While we were in SB yesterday, Helen suddenly missed her necklace. She'd had it on at lunch, so it must have come unfastened sometime during the afternoon.'

'You didn't mention it last night,' Kate remarked.

Recovering herself, Helen said, 'There was no point. Everyone was taken up with the news of Caro's father, and compared with that, it was unimportant.'

'Had it been handed in?' Nicholas asked.

She shook her head. 'No, they didn't hold out much hope.'

'What was it like?' Kate persisted.

'A string of amber beads.' The necklace that had broken, not on Sunday in Steeple Bayliss but on Saturday at Beckworth, leading to her discovery of the button.

'I hope it turns up,' Stella said after a pause, and general conversation resumed. It was some moments before Helen, still filled with relief at her deliverance, realized that by seizing on Michael's explanation, she had tacitly admitted to him that she'd something to hide. He must be wondering what her real reason was for visiting the police.

Helen had underestimated Ledbetter's interest in the horoscopes. Before setting out to bring in Caroline Budd, he called in two young DCs.

'Right, lads, I've a couple of jobs for you. You, Steve, can get down to the library at the *Broadshire News* and check through the last two years of the horoscope column.'

Steve Pembury's eyes widened, but Ledbetter continued: 'They might be on microfilm, they might not, but the job's not as daunting as it sounds. I'm only interested in the entries for "Tomorrow's Birthday", which is given separately. I want you to note the date every time a phrase like "Someone is waiting to hear from you" is used – the words might vary slightly.'

'Didn't know you were interested in the stars, Guv,' Pembury said, straight-faced.

'Watch it. And you, Phil, can get me a list of the dates of all the Stately Home robberies since the first one two years ago. After you've done that, you can join Steve at the *News* and lend a hand. ASAP, both of you.'

Accompanied by WDC Nicky Birch, Ledbetter arrived at the address he'd been given to find a house of mourning. Roderick Budd had died during the night.

A woman friend, imagining they'd come to offer condolences, didn't catch Ledbetter's identification and showed them into a sitting-room. After a few minutes, during which they stood uneasily in the centre of the room, a young woman came in, her eyes red with crying.

'I'm afraid my mother can't see anyone at the moment,' she said. 'It's very kind of you to come; who shall I say called?'

'Miss Caroline Budd?'

She blinked. 'I beg your pardon?'

'Are you Caroline Budd?'

'No, I'm Naomi. Caro's my sister.'

'We'd like to see her, please.'

The girl hesitated. 'Could I ask what it's about? She's very upset at the moment.'

'It's a police matter, Miss Budd. I'm Detective Inspector Ledbetter and this is Constable Birch.'

'Police?' She looked thoroughly bewildered. 'Has she been speeding again? Surely it can wait, in the circumstances. She's not going anywhere.'

Oh yes, she is, Ledbetter thought. Aloud, he said, 'It's rather more serious than that, and we really do need to see her.'

'All right, I'll see if I can find her.'

Another wait, then the door opened and a different girl stood there, smaller and fairer than her sister, with enormous eyes in a pale, pointed face. She didn't speak, simply stood staring at them as though they were some sort of mirage.

Ledbetter cleared his throat. 'Caroline Budd?'

She gave an almost imperceptible nod.

'I'm sorry about your father, Miss Budd, but I must ask you to accompany us to the police station for questioning in connection with the country house burglaries.'

She swayed and Nicky Birch started forward, but the girl had already steadied herself against the door frame.

She moistened her lips and said in a whisper, 'My mother –'

'I'm sure your sister will take care of her,' Ledbetter said firmly. He expected some kind of protest but she said nothing and, doubting if she would take in any formal wording at this stage, he left it unsaid. She could be cautioned before

148

the questioning; in the meantime it was better she should go with them voluntarily.

Twenty minutes later, she was seated opposite him in the chair Helen Campbell had occupied that afternoon. Nicky Birch was at his side.

The time and those present were stated for the tape, then Ledbetter turned to the girl. 'Caroline Budd, I'm cautioning you that you don't have to say anything unless you wish to do so, but anything you do say may be taken down and given in evidence. Do you understand?'

She nodded.

'Would you speak aloud for the tape, please?'

'I understand.'

'I believe you can assist us with our inquiries into the country house burglaries. Would you like to make a statement?'

A pause. Then, 'No.'

'Miss Budd, I think you should know that some officers have gone to London to accompany your friend Dominic Hardy back here.'

She fastened her wide eyes on him and said nothing, though he saw her tremble. He was beginning to find that unwavering stare unnerving. Damn it, it was she who was supposed to be ill at ease.

'You live with Mr Hardy?'

A nod.

'For the tape, please?'

'Yes.'

'Yet he left your parents' home this morning, when your father had just died?'

She spoke her first full sentence in their presence. 'He had an appointment in London.'

Which presumably took precedence over his girlfriend's grief. A never-present help in trouble, Ledbetter thought caustically.

'How long have you known him?'

She said listlessly, 'About four years.'

Abruptly he changed tack. 'Are you interested in antiques, Miss Budd?'

149

Again the widening of the eyes. It was a wonder to Ledbetter that they could open any further: maximum expan-
sion seemed to have been reached several minutes ago.

'Well?'

She said, 'I don't know much about them.'

'Just what you like, eh?'

She did not answer. He sighed. It was some time since
an interview had been such heavy going. He could not tell
whether she was in shock over her father's death or playing
cat and mouse with him. He suspected a mixture of the two.

'Miss Budd, I appreciate that these are difficult circumstances for you, but – '

And then she started to cry. First the gigantic eyes filled
slowly with tears, which brimmed over and began to run
down her cheeks. Then her lip trembled like a child's. Finally,
she laid her arms down on the desk, pillowed her head in
them and gave herself up to a storm of sobbing.

Ledbetter said in an aside, 'We won't get anything out of
her in this condition.' Then, raising his voice, 'All right, Miss
Budd, that's all for now. We'll get the doctor to take a look
at you.' And into the tape, 'Interview suspended at eighteen-
thirty.'

And a hell of a lot of use it had been, he thought in frustration. All they had against her was her association with Hardy
and the reasonable suspicion she'd have benefited from the
crimes. If Hardy had stayed on at the house, things would
have been much easier; as it was, this enforced hanging
around slowed everything almost to a standstill.

He looked at his watch. Dave wouldn't even have got to
London yet; at best it would be an hour and a half before
he could expect his phone-call. In the meantime, they must
hope it wouldn't rain before they could get a look at those
tyre prints.

The journey to London took over two and a half hours, and
it was after eight when Webb and Jackson drew up outside
the luxury apartments where Dominic Hardy lived. The
entrance door was locked and Jackson rang the foyer bell.
After a moment, a voice spoke over the intercom.

150

'Hall porter here.'

'This is the police. May we come in?'

'I'll need to see your identification, sir.'

'Of course.'

Through the plate glass they watched a uniformed man approach over acres of marble floor and peer at the warrant cards they held up. He opened the door and looked at them dubiously.

'What's the problem? One of the residents met with an accident?'

'No, no. We'd like to see Mr Dominic Hardy. Is he in the building?'

'Mr Hardy? No, sir. He arrived back after the weekend, garaged his car, left his suitcase for me to take upstairs, and went straight out again.'

'What time was that?'

'Mid-morning I'd say.'

'And he hasn't been back since?'

'No, but that's not unusual. He often goes straight on to dinner from work, and sometimes to a show or a club after that.'

'Great!' Jackson said under his breath.

'Is this the entrance he'd use?'

'Yes, sir, since he hasn't got the car with him. When he has, he comes up in the lift from the garage level.'

Webb thought for a moment. 'And you've no idea when to expect him?'

'No, sir.'

'Then we shall have to wait. Is there a restaurant in the building?'

'Yes, along the hall there, but it's only for residents and their guests.'

'We don't want to go in,' Webb said impatiently, 'but I'd be glad if you'd arrange for some sandwiches to be sent out to us. We'll be in the car parked at the kerb.'

'Oh, I don't think —' The porter broke off under Webb's gimlet gaze. 'I'll see what I can do, sir.'

'Thank you. Two rounds, and something to drink if possible — tea or coffee.'

The porter did not look happy. Unused to his establishment being used as a transport café, he was doubtless anticipating the receipt of his request by an irate chef.

Webb said, 'And if by any chance Mr Hardy should phone, I'd be grateful if you didn't mention we're here.'

In silence the porter opened the door, waited as they went through, and locked it behind them.

'Good thinking on the sandwiches, Guv,' Jackson said with relief. 'I was beginning to wonder when we could eat.'

'I know, Ken, I was getting your vibes. They're more likely to be smoked salmon than cheese and pickle, but beggars can't be choosers.'

In fact, the sandwiches, brought out to them ten minutes later by a young waiter, contained slices of rare beef. Also on the tray were paper napkins, a jar of English mustard, sugar bowl, cream jug and two cups of coffee. The bill was folded discreetly and tucked under a plate.

Jackson was impressed. 'Hope Chummie doesn't come back till we've finished this lot,' he commented.

Webb glanced at the bill, gave a low whistle and tucked it away again. Just as well he could put it on expenses.

Twenty minutes later, the performance with the hall porter was repeated when Jackson took back the tray and, funded by Webb, settled the bill. It was confirmed that Mr Hardy had not phoned in.

On receipt of this information, Webb reached for his own phone and called the number Ledbetter had given him.

'He's not shown up yet, Chris. We're parked outside the apartment building and he's definitely not inside. The hall porter says he often dines out and goes on to a show, so God knows when he'll get back. But since he can't be contacted at the apartment, I'd say you're safe enough to let the SOCOs get under way.'

Ledbetter swore softly. 'Wouldn't you know it? OK, Dave, thanks, I'll do that. Hope you're not kept waiting too long.'

'You picked up the girlfriend?'

'Yep.' He did not elaborate, and Webb let it go.

'I'll ring back when we've got him,' he said, and switched off the phone. Then, selecting a cassette, he slid it into the slot and, with Jackson beside him, settled down for a long wait.

When dinner was over, Helen was anxious not to be alone with Michael. He might well consider, after his rescue of her, that he was entitled to hear the real reason for her visit to the police. Throughout the meal she had been trying to think of an innocent explanation; the trouble was that if it had been innocent, she would not have hesitated to reveal it in the first place.

Something to do with Andrew, perhaps? That would account for not wanting to broadcast it, but she could think of nothing remotely convincing.

Seeing Terry Pike make for the television lounge, Helen thankfully followed him. She didn't like the man, and he had caused the embarrassment in the first place, but he was unlikely to refer back to it.

He turned as she closed the door behind her. 'Anything in particular you want to watch?'

'Only the news, and it's not quite time yet.'

He switched the set on and they both sat down. Helen's ear was attuned for Michael's arrival, but he did not come. Having appeared to be on her side, was he now conferring with the others about what might be the true reason for her contacting the police? Yet, she reminded herself, it was she who had tried to avoid him. Perhaps he'd noticed and was simply keeping out of her way.

She leant her head back and, ignoring the flickering screen, closed her eyes. There were suddenly so many questions in her life – Andrew and that woman, the tensions that had built up here over the week, her attitude to Michael and his to her. It had taken Pen to bring this last to her notice, but she admitted now that she found him attractive.

A familiar fanfare intruded on her musings, and at the same moment Terry said, 'Wake up, Sleeping Beauty, the news is starting.'

They watched it in silence for some ten minutes, until raised voices in the hall attracted their attention.

Terry said, 'What the hell's going on?' and went to open

the door. Helen followed him in time to hear Stella demand shrilly, 'But what are they *doing* here? Don't they have to have a warrant or something?'

Helen felt herself go hot. The police?

'What's happening?' Terry demanded, and Stella made an obvious attempt to calm down.

'The high-handed arm of the law,' she said. 'They're rigging up arc lights outside – God knows why.'

'Outside where?'

'At the front. Gordon and Nicholas are out there trying to find out what's going on. Kate says they're taking photographs.'

'Of what, for Pete's sake?'

'How should I know?' Her voice had started to rise again. 'There's only gravel and shrubs out there.'

Helen thought suddenly: It's where I told them Dominic parked his car.

Almost as though reading her mind, Terry said softly, 'Well, well, you're having a surfeit of the police today, aren't you, Helen? Perhaps they're looking for your necklace.'

She said stiffly, 'I hardly think it warrants arc lamps.'

The front door opened and Nicholas and Gordon came back inside, slapping their arms for warmth. Kate, who had been waiting at the door, said quickly, 'Did you get any more out of them?'

'No, we were told to keep back, if you please. Damn it, it's our property, we're entitled to an explanation.'

'They were very polite,' Nicholas put in. 'Assured us they didn't want to come into the house or disturb us in any way.'

'They *are* disturbing us,' Stella said.

Nicholas's eyes had gone past her to Helen, standing rigidly by the door to the television room.

'If they want to make mud pies, I can't see there's any objection,' he said.

Kate stared at him. 'Is that what they're doing?'

'That's what it looked like to me. After all of which, I could do with a drink. Anyone care to join me?'

Uncertainly they moved towards the bar, but Helen had had enough of their company. There was no saying how long it would be before another barbed comment referred back to her visit to the police station. The stairs lay between her and the bar; unnoticed, she ran up them and turned into the corridor. To come face to face with Michael.

She could only guess at the expression on her face, because he put a hand out and said quickly, 'Hey, it's me! I'm not going to bite you!'

She laughed shakily. 'Sorry.'

'You're a bundle of nerves, aren't you? Ever since we met that blasted husband of yours.'

When she made no reply, he said, 'Do you know what's going on outside? I've been watching from my window.'

'I think it's the police.' She added foolishly, 'Nicholas said they're making mud pies.'

'Is it your doing?'

She looked up at him, heart leaping. 'What do you mean?'

'Helen, you're always asking me what I mean. It was a simple enough question. However, this is no place to talk; my room's just here.' And, as she drew back, he added acidly, 'You needn't worry, I shan't compromise you.'

He had the knack of putting her in the wrong. Discomfited, she would have made some excuse, but he'd taken her arm and was opening the door beside them. The room was smaller than she expected – one of the two singles Stella had mentioned that first evening. It was also brilliantly lit by the lights which streamed through the uncurtained window.

Helen walked across and looked down. The whole scene was illuminated by the hard, white light, as though actors were taking part in a play. As Nicholas had said, two men were on their hands and knees on the ground, while others held cameras. Their concentration was almost palpable and Helen was thankful it wasn't she they were after.

Michael came to join her and they stood watching in silence.

'You know what they're doing, don't you?' he said at last. 'Or are you going to deny that as well?'

She said indignantly, 'I haven't denied anything.'

'Well, profess ignorance then. Same difference.' And at her continuing silence, he went on, 'Right, then I'll spell it out for you. They're examining the ground where Dominic's car was parked last night.'

'But why?'

He seemed taken aback by her genuine bewilderment. 'For tyre prints, I imagine, since they appear to be taking casts.'

'But why should they want casts of Dominic's tyre prints?'

'At a guess, to compare them with prints they already have.' He paused. 'And who knows where they obtained those?'

She turned slowly to face him. 'Michael, do you know what this is all about?'

'My dear girl, you appear to know far more than I do. I've been staying here peacefully for several months now, and nothing struck me as being amiss. But no sooner do you arrive than tensions mount and we have the police sniffing around. Are you going to tell me why you really went to them this afternoon?'

She said awkwardly, 'I haven't thanked you for helping me out.'

'You were so obviously floundering, and on a flash of inspiration, I noticed you weren't wearing the beads you'd had on earlier in the week. Don't, for God's sake, wear them again. Terry's office is in Maybury Street, by the way; he must have seen you from his window.

'So, are you going to enlighten me? Or,' he added, his voice hardening, 'do you still not trust me?'

'It's not that,' she said – though it was, in part. 'It's just that it's all wild speculation as far as I'm concerned and I can't start slandering people till I have some kind of proof.'

'But you had enough to go to the police.'

'I had enough,' she corrected him, 'to want to hand the responsibility over to them and let them sort it out.'

'And that's all you're going to tell me?'

'For the moment, yes.'

'Helen Campbell, there are times when I want to shake you.' He paused. 'And there are also times when I want to do something quite different.' Another pause. 'And the worst times are when I want to do both things at once, such as now.'

She stood very still, her eyes on his face.

'You see, until yesterday I thought you were a happily married woman, and that the bond which seemed to be growing between us must remain a surface one. But you're not happily married, are you?'

She said barely audibly, 'Not at the moment, no.'

'You're going back to him at the end of the week?'

'Yes.'

'Whether or not that woman turns out to be his mistress?'

'I have to go back, Michael, at least to discuss it.'

'And if she is?'

Her eyes dropped. 'I don't know.'

'All right. I've said more than enough, but I just want you to know that if you need a shoulder to cry on, mine's available. Now, perhaps you'd better go, before I forget my promise not to compromise you.'

She said with difficulty, 'Thank you for being so understanding.'

He gave a harsh laugh. 'Understanding is the last thing I am. I've not the slightest idea what's going on, but I *am* worried that you might be putting yourself in danger. If you won't let me help you, at least promise me you'll take care of yourself.'

'I promise,' she said. She reached up and lightly kissed his cheek. 'Good night, Michael.'

And leaving him standing looking after her, she let herself out of the room.

13

'Guv!'

Jackson's excited voice jolted Webb from the strains of a piano concerto and he straightened swiftly.

'There's a bloke getting out of a taxi – is that him?'

Webb looked across at the man bent to the taxi-driver's window.

'Very probably, Ken. Let's go and find out.'

They caught up with him as he was about to insert his key in the entrance door of the building.

'Mr Hardy?'

He spun round at the sound of Webb's voice, and for a moment Jackson thought he was going to make a dash for it. But he just paused and waited.

'DCI Webb and Sergeant Jackson, Shillingham CID.'

Hardy said softly, 'Slightly off your patch, aren't you, gentlemen?'

'I'm arresting you on suspicion of aggravated burglary in connection with country houses, and must ask you to accompany us back to Broadshire. I'm also cautioning you, sir. You understand what that means?'

'Oh, I do, Chief Inspector, I do.'

He turned without demur and went with them back to the car. 'Been waiting long?' he asked conversationally, as Webb handcuffed him to Jackson and gestured him into the back.

'Long enough.'

Webb got into the driver's seat and checked the dashboard clock. It was eleven-thirty-two. He reached for the phone in the glove compartment.

'Chris? We're on our way.'

*   *   *

Maybury Street police station was the only building in Steeple Bayliss that showed any lights. Night and day were interchangeable here and the fact that it was two-fifteen in the morning made no difference to the bustling sense of purpose.

Ledbetter was waiting for them in the foyer and Webb went to have a private word with him.

'He's been chatting happily all the way home,' he reported. 'You'd have thought he was at a bloody cocktail party. Nothing relevant, mind. A blow-by-blow account of a play he saw last week, the state of English rugby, the best way to cook grouse. I wished to God he'd shut up, but at least it passed the time.'

'Nerves, would you say?'

'Could be, but if so they're well disguised.' Webb paused. 'Did the girlfriend cough?'

'No. Her father's just died and we finished up having to give her a sedative. She's asleep in the doctor's room.' He jerked his head towards Hardy, standing chatting to an unresponsive Jackson. 'Does he know we've got her?'

'Not from us.'

'Fine. OK, then, here we go. Want to sit in on it?'

'You bet I do. But Ken Jackson's out on his feet; is there anywhere he can get his head down?'

'Sure, I'll get someone to show him the way. You must be pretty exhausted yourself. I at least managed a brief nap while I was waiting.'

'I shan't sleep till I know whether this lad's behind the country house business, so let's get on with it.'

All the same, he was grateful for the strong black coffee that was brought to the interview room. Ledbetter switched on the tape and went through the usual procedure. Then he took a small plastic envelope from his pocket and pushed it across to Hardy. As far as Webb could see, it contained a small gold button.

Hardy's eyes fastened on it, but he made no move to pick it up.

'Yours, I believe,' Ledbetter said.

'Not necessarily, Inspector. All members of my club wear them.'

'Nevertheless, if you were to look at the sleeve of your blazer, I believe you'd find one missing.'

Hardy's eyes narrowed. 'And why the hell should you think that?'

'Because this is smaller than the breast buttons. And also because you're the only member of Chardsey Yacht Club whom we know to have visited the area.'

'What area are we talking about?'

'Beckworth House.'

'Then I'm afraid you're mistaken; I've never visited Beckworth.'

'You might also be interested to know that we have taken casts of your tyre prints from outside the Seven Stars guesthouse to compare with those found near Buckhurst Grange on the night of the break-in.'

'How very enterprising of you.'

'Some hairs were also found at the scene. It will be interesting if we can complete the hat-trick by matching them to yours.'

'You have been busy bees. Any other little snippets I should know?'

'Only that your girlfriend's here.'

A flash of something Webb couldn't analyse rippled across Hardy's face and was gone. That got to him, he thought.

'What have you done to her?' The bantering note had left his voice.

'We had an interesting chat,' Ledbetter lied.

'That was bloody insensitive of you, when her father's just died.'

'Lord Cleverley died on Thursday,' Webb said without expression.

The colour left Hardy's face, but his voice was tightly controlled. 'The significance of that comment eludes me.'

'Just an observation, sir,' Webb said stolidly. 'In the midst of life, and all that.'

'I don't need reminding, thank you. Like Charles II,

Roderick took an unconscionable time dying, and I don't mind telling you it got me down.'

'Which was why you deserted the grieving family and went back to London?'

He said with a flash of anger, 'Caro never said that!'

'I'm saying it, Mr Hardy.'

'Then what *did* Caro say?'

'Suppose you tell us your side of it.'

For what seemed several minutes but was probably only seconds, the two men held each other's eyes, weighing each other up, perhaps calling each other's bluff. Then, unexpectedly, Hardy relaxed and sat back in his chair.

'Oh, what the hell?' he said. 'If the game's up, at least we had a good run for our money.'

Webb and Ledbetter exchanged a quick look. Could it be as easy as that?

Ledbetter said, 'You're prepared to make a statement?'

'I suppose so, since you've doubtless wormed most of it out of Caro; she'd have been in no state to stand up to your "chat".' He said the word viciously. 'Before we go any further, though, I must make one thing clear. Lord Cleverley's death was an accident and we bitterly regret it. I met him once at a polo match; he was a nice old chap.'

'Which didn't stop you hitting him over the head to save your skin.'

Hardy looked quickly from one to the other. 'Hold on a minute. What exactly did Caro tell you?'

'What are *you* telling us, Mr Hardy?'

'Do you know, Inspector, I think you've pulled a fast one. You *haven't* got a statement from Caro, have you?'

'I never said we had.'

'Bloody hell!' Hardy said softly. 'The oldest trick in the book, and I fell for it!' Then, surprisingly, he laughed.

'All right, you win. If you've got this far, I'm not going to demean myself by squirming. What do you want to know?'

'Everything,' Ledbetter said promptly, 'but principally where the stolen goods went and how we can get them back.'

'Ah, now I'm afraid I can't help you there. I know nothing of the business arrangements.'

Webb's heart plummeted. It seemed that even with Hardy's cooperation, things weren't after all going to be that easy.

'Then what did you do with them?' he demanded.

'Deposited them at the Seven Stars for onward transit.'

The detectives tried to hide their surprise. Webb thought, so Chris was right; there is a connection. Ledbetter spared a quick, silent cheer for Mrs Campbell.

'How did you decide which to rob and what to take?'

'Explicit orders from Nicholas Warren. I did the necessary, delivered the goods, and received a handsome payment for my trouble. In cash.'

'So Nicholas Warren's behind it all?'

'Come, now, Inspector, I'm not going to do all your work for you. That's up to you to find out.'

Webb said, 'Tell me one thing: why in the name of heaven did you sometimes ignore the equivalent of the Crown Jewels and take some worthless trinket?'

Hardy shrugged. 'It was immaterial to me what we took. We stole directly to order – no more and no less. And the payment was as good for the trinkets as for the more expensive items, so who was I to quibble?'

'You said "we". Miss Budd was in on it with you?'

'This is where I should be gallant and deny it, but there seems little point. Of course she was. She's petite and agile and could get into small spaces that I couldn't. She was invaluable.'

'And I presume,' Ledbetter said quietly, 'that it was she who killed Lord Cleverley?'

'I gave that away, didn't I? But it was an accident, as I said. I was across the room looking at that shepherdess and wondering, I admit, why anyone should pay such a tidy sum for me to nick it, when suddenly the door opened and the old man came in in his dressing-gown. We got the fright of our lives, I can tell you. And Caro, who was behind the door, picked up a candlestick and hit him with it. He went down like the proverbial ton of bricks. It was a purely instinctive gesture – self defence, really.'

'Except that he had to be stopped from identifying you.'

'Caro didn't know that at the time – that we'd met, I mean. When we heard he'd died, she went completely to pieces. Coming on top of her father's illness, it knocked the stuffing out of her.'

There was a short silence, while the three of them thought over what had been said. Then Webb asked, 'How did it all start? Did this Warren ring you up out of the blue and invite you to embark on a series of burglaries for him?'

'Not exactly.' Hardy paused to massage the back of his neck with one hand. It occurred to Webb that he too had had a long day. 'We were at school together,' he went on, 'though I was a year or two younger. I had a somewhat notorious reputation, always in hot water for breaking some rule or other. I was hooked on the Raffles books – "the gentleman thief", you know – and I started practising steal-ing from people. Only as an exercise, I hasten to add; I always returned what I took; it was just to prove that I could, though it didn't always go down too well, and eventually, what with one thing and another, I was expelled.

'Well, the years rolled on, and the next time our paths crossed was in South Africa. We met at a party and exchanged the time of day – we'd never been close friends. Then, to my surprise, he phoned a couple of days later and suggested we met for a drink.

'The root of it was that a diplomatic crisis was brewing; the wife of a government official had had a piece of jewellery stolen, and swore she knew who'd taken it. But this other woman's husband was also a high-ranking official, and all hell would have broken out if she'd accused her publicly. And having just met me again, Nicholas remembered my doings at school, and asked if I'd be prepared to try to steal it back.

'Well, of course, I was delighted, and nicked it with the greatest of ease. And the beauty of it was that the woman couldn't make a fuss, because she wasn't supposed to have it in the first place. Nicholas sent me a case of champagne and returned the brooch to its owner to the acclaim of all concerned. It did his career no harm at all, I can tell you; he became quite a folk hero in his clique.'

Ledbetter stood up, stretched, and went to the door to request more coffee.

'So when you both came back to this country,' he said as he sat down again, 'you dreamed up the country house scam?'

'Again, not exactly; I had no part in dreaming up anything. But as you say, he contacted me again, and asked how I'd feel about trying my hand on a larger scale. I was intrigued – life in the City can be pretty dull and I'm all for a bit of excitement. And because I moved in well-heeled circles, I was able to case the stately joints without arousing suspicion. Raffles again. It worked like a dream.'

'And you have no idea what Nicholas Warren did with the spoils?'

'Not a clue, though if it's any help, I'm damn sure the substantial payments didn't come out of his pocket.'

The fresh coffee arrived and they drank it in silence.

'Warren's brother-in-law writes horoscopes for the *Evening News*, doesn't he?' Ledbetter said then.

Hardy raised a quizzical eyebrow. 'Does he? Good Lord!'

'You didn't know that?'

'No; any reason why I should?'

Ledbetter did not reply. Hardy had nothing to gain from lying at this stage, and Mrs Campbell said they were sensitive about the column. It was possible they didn't mention the connection, even to friends.

So although the Seven Stars was up to its neck in all this, no direct connection had yet been made with the horoscopes, which were what had roused Mrs Campbell's suspicions in the first place. Perhaps he'd know more when he had Steve Pembury's report.

He looked at Hardy. 'Anything you'd like to add to your statement?'

'Come, come, Inspector; you've already got jam on it!'

Ledbetter couldn't help smiling. In other circumstances, this was a man he could have admired.

'In that case, interview terminated at three-twenty.' He switched off the tape. 'Your statement will be typed in the morning. I'll see you then.'

They waited till Hardy had been led away to the cells. 'Right, home, James, and don't spare the horses. The guest-room bed's made up, and knowing Janet, she'll probably insist on cooking us bacon and eggs before we crash out.'

'Sounds great,' Webb said, getting stiffly to his feet. 'My round of sandwiches at eight-thirty seems a long time ago.'

Together they went out into the cold, starlit night.

Some seven hours later, five police cars drew up outside the Seven Stars. Ledbetter and Hopkins approached the door, the other officers remaining in the vehicles.

Their ring was answered by a tall, red-haired woman.

'What is it? What's happened?' she demanded, before they could speak.

'SB CID, ma'am. Detective Inspector Ledbetter and DS Hopkins. And you are –?'

'Stella Cain.'

'We'd like a word with you all.'

Stella's eyes went past him to the vehicles lined up on the gravel. 'Five cars? But what –'

'The others are in, I hope?' Ledbetter interrupted.

'Yes,' Stella admitted hesitantly, and after a moment held the door open for them to enter. 'My sister and brother-in-law are in their apartment.' She gestured towards one of the wings which extended on either side of the front door.

'Perhaps you'd tell them we're here.' Though, Ledbetter thought, they could scarcely have failed to notice their arrival. Sure enough, at Mrs Cain's knock, the door to the wing opened immediately and a tall, grey-haired man came out, closely followed by his wife.

'Nicholas Warren?'

'Who wants to know?'

'Inspector Ledbetter, Steeple Bayliss CID. And you, ma'am: could I have your full name?'

She stared at him with unflinching dark eyes. 'Katherine Warren.'

'Nicholas and Katherine Warren, I'm arresting you on sus-picion of conspiracy to burgle and handling stolen goods. You're not obliged to say anything, but anything you do say may be taken down and used in evidence. Do you understand?'

The man looked stunned. His wife, clutching his arm, stood immobile.

'Do you both understand?' Ledbetter repeated.

They nodded.

'You'll be taken separately to the station for questioning.' He nodded to Hopkins, who opened the front door and signalled to his colleagues.

As the Warrens were escorted out of the house, Ledbetter turned to Mrs Cain, still standing like a mesmerized rabbit in the middle of the hall. 'Now, ma'am, where's your husband?'

'In his study,' she answered mechanically.

He gestured to her to lead the way and they walked in silence through the large kitchen, where preparations for the evening meal had been interrupted by their arrival, out of the back door and across the courtyard to the mews buildings. Mrs Cain pushed open a door and called up the stairs, 'Gordon! Can you come down?'

There was the sound of a chair being pushed back and Cain appeared at the top of the stairs, stopping short as he saw the detectives. Slowly, resignedly, he came down, to be arrested with his wife on the same charges as the others.

As they walked back to the house, Stella said anxiously, 'Will we be back this afternoon? We have guests, who'll be expecting a meal.'

'Arrangements will be made,' Ledbetter answered enigmatically. 'In the meantime, I have a warrant to search the premises.'

'Now look here –' Cain burst out angrily, then broke off with a helpless shrug of his shoulders. Two officers were waiting in the hall to accompany them, also in separate cars, back to the station.

'And now,' Ledbetter said with satisfaction, 'they can all kick their heels while we see what we can find here. Tell the rest of the lads to come in, Happy.'

At Melbray the Old Masters lecture was in full swing, amply illustrated by colourful slides. It should have been one of the highlights of the week, but Helen was finding it hard to concentrate.

Had the police found what they were looking for last night? Was Dominic really involved with the Stately Homes break-ins? If so, was it her conversation with Inspector Ledbetter that had led them to him? And how would Andrew react at her involvement in what he'd regarded as his private investigation?

And Michael. Time and again she went over what had been said in his room. If things didn't work out with Andrew, would she contact him? Did she *want* things to work out, or, having made this tentative break, would she prefer to extend it indefinitely?

To none of these questions had she any answers, but the weight of them was bringing on a migraine. She gritted her teeth. She'd paid for this course, and it was laying the foundation of her future. She couldn't afford to allow personal worries to affect her concentration.

But the worries intruded again at lunch-time, when, told someone was waiting to see her, she found a young woman in the foyer.

'Mrs Campbell? I'm WDC Birch. Mr Ledbetter asked me to tell you that the two couples from the Seven Stars are at the station, and though they're likely to be released later, he thought you might be uncomfortable staying on there.'

Helen swallowed. 'You mean he told them I – ?'

'No, no, but apparently you'd shown some interest in horoscopes, and when the subject was brought up, Mrs Warren immediately assumed you were involved. It seems they knew of your visit to the station.'

Suspicious Kate, and Terry, with his prying eyes. Well, if she was to be a – grass, was that the word? – she might as well go all the way.

'I mentioned Mr Pike, one of the lodgers, to the inspector. I think he might be worth talking to as well.'

'I'll see he gets the message. In the meantime, if you would like to move, I can run you back to the Seven Stars and help you pack up your things before they get back. There are several good B & B places in town – I'm sure you'll have no difficulty finding one.'

Webb had returned to Shillingham that morning to write up a report on a case he'd been dealing with. By mid-afternoon he'd finished it, and, curious to know how things were progressing, he phoned Ledbetter.

'Dave – I was just about to ring you. We've had quite a profitable day, one way or another. Know what we found in a safe at the Seven Stars? One Nymphenberg shepherdess.'

'That's all?' He'd been expecting an Aladdin's cave.

''Fraid so, everything else has been passed on.'

'And the sixty-four-thousand-dollar question,' Webb said, 'is to whom?'

'Yes, but unfortunately we don't have the sixty-four-thousand-dollar answer. Look, it's too involved to go into on the phone. Can you get over here?'

'Should think so. I've been on to Regional Crime, by the way and put them in the picture. Shall I bring Brian Rigby along?'

'Sure. You can both listen to the tapes if you like.'

'Are the Seven Stars lot still with you?'

'No, released on bail. There's not much against the women, anyway, other than benefiting from the proceeds of crime. They haven't been charged.'

'Fair enough. See you in about an hour, then.'

Helen had asked at the desk for a copy of the accommodations list before leaving Melbray. There were three or four addresses in Steeple Bayliss; she picked one at random and rang to ask if they'd a free room, explaining she would need it for four nights. They had, and directions were given how to get there.

Now, feeling lonely and bereft, she stood in the middle of it and looked about her. It had nothing like the atmosphere of the poppy-and-cream bedroom at the Seven Stars, being small and dark, with a single, high window looking out on to a brick wall.

Still, she told herself, she would be spared the smouldering atmosphere and suspicious glances.

She'd left a cheque at the guesthouse covering the full fortnight, together with a brief note saying she was moving to be closer to her daughter. They'd know, of course, that was not the reason for her flight; doubtless it would cause sardonic amusement.

And Michael . . . She drew in her breath sharply, realizing for the first time that he might take her precipitate departure as a direct result of their conversation last night.

She stood stricken, hands clasped in front of her. What could she do? Certainly not phone him at the Seven Stars, and she didn't know where he worked. Oh, why hadn't she thought to slip a note under his door? Though under the eyes of the efficient young policewoman, that might have been difficult.

It was the horoscopes that had brought her to this, she reflected; if she'd confined herself to handing over the button, Dominic would have been arrested (as the police-woman told her he had been) and no one would have connected her with the betrayal. But as soon as Ledbetter had mentioned horoscopes – and he must have placed more importance on them than she'd realized – Kate would have known she was behind it.

So here she was, displaced and alone and desperately in need of someone to talk to. But it was only two days since she'd seen Pen, and she mustn't keep making demands on her time. She was still telling herself this as she went down to the public call-box and dialled the halls of residence.

'Just to let you know I've changed my phone number,' she said brightly, when her daughter came on the line. 'In case you wanted to fix that meal.'

'What do you mean, you've –?' Penelope broke off and her voice sharpened. 'Have you left the Seven Stars?'

'Yes,' Helen admitted, keeping an eye on the half-closed door to the kitchen, from which a somewhat unappetizing smell of supper was emerging.

'But why? Did they throw you out?'

'Certainly not! I'll explain when I see you.'

'Mum, you can't leave it at that! Did you go on poking your nose in and get their backs up? What *happened*? And where are you now?'

'At a B & B in town, on one of the roads overlooking the river.' She hesitated, but loneliness overcame her resolve not to make demands. 'Could you possibly slip out for an hour?'

'Of course I could. Shall we meet at the Barley Mow? It shouldn't be far from you, and I can bike down.'

'That would be lovely,' Helen said gratefully. 'Seven-thirty?' She'd been informed that 'tea' was served at six, and the evening had stretched interminably ahead. There would be no interesting conversation over the dining-table here.

'I'll be there,' Penelope said.

14

Brian Rigby was a small, sharp-featured man, with a penchant for telling old jokes. Webb, who liked him well enough, was nevertheless relieved when they drew up in front of Maybury Street police station and he was spared having to force any more laughs.

It was five o'clock, the rush-hour traffic was under way, and he wondered how it would feel to know exactly what time you'd be home each evening. Boring, he decided, pushing his way through the swing doors. It did not seem all that long since he'd arrived here in the early hours with Dominic Hardy. Now the case had moved forward again, though it seemed their principal quarry still eluded them.

'So what had they all to say for themselves?' Webb asked Ledbetter, when they were seated in his office.

'I saw Warren first. Once he realized the game was up, he confirmed Hardy's story of the stolen brooch. The circumstances of its recovery became quite a legend, and eventually reached the ears of the man he refers to as Q.'

'Why Q?' Webb asked.

'It stands for "Query", since Warren didn't know his name. And,' Ledbetter ended flatly, 'I regret to say, still doesn't.'

Webb slammed his hand on the arm of the chair. 'You're not telling me that even now we don't know who's behind it?'

'That's exactly what I'm telling you,' Ledbetter said grimly. 'Anyway, to continue. After he came back from South Africa, Warren had a phone call. The caller said he'd learned of his feat in retrieving the brooch and wondered if he'd like to put his expertise to further use. Warren explained he hadn't

171

recovered it himself, but agreed to contact his colleague.

'And that was the start of it. Once Hardy agreed to come in, the operation took shape, but the damnable thing is that after all this time, Q is still an enigma and Warren has no way of contacting him.

'He's the sole instigator. Warren receives a phone-call – always on a Wednesday evening at eight o'clock – and is told what item is desired. Sometimes Q doesn't even know where it is – he might just have read about it, or seen it illustrated in a magazine.

'Those, believe it or not, are the cases Warren enjoys most. Strategy and planning are his forté and he admits he was finding life dull back in this country. There's never any time-limit imposed, and sometimes he plans several "easier" thefts while working on what he regards as a challenging, long-term one. Once, he said, it took him a full year to discover who owned a certain vase and where it was, and then work out the means of acquiring it. Honestly, Dave, to hear him talk, you'd think he was businessman of the year!

'Once Hardy has stolen the item and delivered it to the Seven Stars, a line is inserted in the horoscope column of the *Evening News* under "Tomorrow's Birthday".'

'What is this about a horoscope column?' Webb interrupted. 'The first time I heard of it was when you mentioned it to Hardy last night.'

Ledbetter explained about Helen Campbell's visit. 'If there's any reward going for nailing this gang, she's the one who should get it,' he ended. 'She spotted the repetitions in the column and she found the lost button at Beckworth. She deserves a gold medal. What puzzled her was why the two parties didn't simply phone each other, but we now have the answer. Warren couldn't contact Q, because he didn't know who he was. The column was the ideal point of contact.

'Q, who obviously lives within the circulation area of the *Evening News*, reads "Tomorrow's Birthday" every day, and when the agreed code appears, phones the following Wednesday with instructions where to take the goods. It's always a postal sorting office, using the poste restante facility, and always a busy one, where staff aren't likely to remember one particular transaction.

'What surprised me is that Warren didn't express any curiosity about the bloke behind it all. He was happy just to be utilizing his strategic skills and being handsomely paid for so doing.'

'What about the payout?' Rigby asked. 'How is it received?'

'By registered post, in wads of fifty-pound notes. It's incredible really, the web of secrecy they maintained: Q knows Warren's identity, but not that of Hardy or Budd. Warren knows Hardy and Budd but not Q; and Hardy and Budd know of Warren's involvement, but not Q's. They didn't even know about the horoscope column, as we discovered last night. So Warren's the kingpin round which it all revolves, the only one known to both sides.'

'What was Cain's part in all this?'

'Minimal. He saw to the horoscopes, of course, and took a small – I gather very small – share in the payout. He also delivered the goods; once the object was in their hands, Warren seemed to lose interest. Incidentally, I had one of my DCs go through the column for the last two years and note the dates when this cryptic message was inserted. In every case it was less than a week after a country house break-in.'

Webb moved impatiently. 'But what happens now, if there's no way of contacting the bugger?'

'Ah, but there is! At least, I hope so. As we know to our cost, there was a robbery at Buckhurst last Thursday, and even after the business with Lord Cleverley, the stolen ornament was delivered to the Seven Stars as usual. Furthermore, one of the agreed phrases appeared in last night's column.'

There was a short silence. Then Webb said, 'So if all goes according to plan, our mystery man should phone at eight tomorrow evening?'

'Exactly. The one fear is that Lord Cleverley's death might have frightened him off, and since the figurine isn't valuable anyway, he could decide not to claim it. In fact, with a murder hunt in progress, he might well think the game isn't worth the candle, resolve to be content with what he has,

173

and retire from the scene completely. In which case we'll never catch up with him.'

'Don't even imagine it!' Rigby said vehemently.

'We can but hope. We've arranged to insert a bugging device in the phone at the guesthouse and with luck the message will come through as usual.'

'Warren will cooperate?'

'He hasn't much option. Our lads will be in a van outside, listening in. The phone-calls are always brief, just the address of the sorting office and the day the parcel has to be delivered.'

'What kind of voice has he got, this Q? Any clues there?'

'He speaks in a whisper – impossible to identify and no discernible accent. So there we have it. Would you like to hear the tapes?'

Webb shook his head and got to his feet. 'You've told me all I need to know. Best of luck with the phone-call. You'll keep us advised?'

'Of course.' Ledbetter stood up. 'I'll come down with you; there's nothing more I can do this evening, so I'm off home. Last night's lack of sleep is catching up with me.'

'Me too,' Webb agreed.

They went through the swing doors to discover it was raining.

'At least there's no evidence it can wash away now,' Ledbetter commented and, raising his hand in a salute, he went on his way.

Helen lay in the narrow, unfamiliar bed, thinking over the evening. In the bar at the Barley Mow, with the rain rattling against the porthole beside them, she and Pen had had the frankest conversation of their lives.

It started, of course, with an account of Helen's visit to the police and the dramatic events that resulted from it.

'So you were right after all, Miss Marple. Well done you!'

'Up to a point, but I was quite wrong about the hit-and-run – it was an accident after all. And a particularly sad one.' Her face clouded.

'Poor Molly; I learned today why she went running out

like that – the inspector asked the policewoman to tell me. It seems she'd overheard them saying some money was missing and wondering if she'd pinched it. The awful thing was that they'd simply miscalculated and discovered the mistake later. Nicholas told the inspector that his main regret in the whole affair was that Molly'd died thinking she was under suspicion.'

Gradually, as the evening passed, their talk had become more personal. Helen had been startled to discover how much Penelope, and by definition Thomas also, had known of the tensions between their parents, which she thought she'd successfully concealed; surprised, also, by the maturity her daughter showed in discussing them.

'We felt so helpless,' she said, 'watching you both rub each other raw and not being able to do anything. We've been expecting for years to hear you were separating.'

'How would you feel if we did?' Helen asked in a low voice.

'Sad, of course, but it wouldn't be the end of the world. We love you both and would keep in touch, so don't stay together simply for our sake. It's much more important to sort out your lives and do what's best for you.' Penelope reached for her hand. 'You saw that woman on Sunday, didn't you?'

Helen nodded.

'I – think I've seen her before.'

Helen looked up sharply. 'Where?'

'I've been trying to remember.'

'With Daddy, you mean?'

'Not exactly with him, but on the fringes. Like Sunday.'

'She must be adept at dodging round corners,' Helen said bitterly.

'What about Michael Saxton, Mum? You do like him, don't you?'

'I like him, but I don't suppose I'll ever see him again.'

'Would you mind if you didn't?'

Helen said lightly, 'I'd be sorry, but after all we've only known each other ten days.'

'What difference does that make? You know something?

175

You were more relaxed with him that I've seen you in years.'

'Only because he's an outsider and I didn't have to keep up pretences.'

Penelope laughed. 'Have it your own way. Anyway, it's great that you're thinking of going back to work full time. After being a wife and mother all these years, you'll be a person in your own right again. And take Sir Clifford up on his offer of help, too. A personal contact like that is worth something.'

Yes, she'd do that, Helen thought, pulling the pillow into the hollow of her neck. These two weeks had been more traumatic than she'd ever anticipated, but at least she'd established contact with Sir Clifford, which should stand her in good stead. She reached up and switched off the light.

Terry Pike settled himself in a chair opposite Ledbetter and commented, 'I suppose I owe this pleasure to Helen Snoopy Campbell?'

'We're interviewing everyone at the Seven Stars, sir,' Ledbetter said smoothly. 'I understand you've been lodging there for some time?'

'A couple of months, but I doubt if it'll be for much longer.'

'Oh?'

'My business should be wrapped up shortly.'

'And what is your business, Mr Pike?'

Pike met and held his eye. 'I'm a private investigator.'

Ledbetter raised an eyebrow. 'Engaged by whom?'

'An insurance company anxious to end the Stately Home break-ins before it goes out of business.'

Ledbetter considered that for a moment. 'I believe you live in the north of England?'

'I do, thank God.'

'I'm just wondering why, since the burglaries have taken place all over the country, you couldn't have operated equally well from there?'

Pike tapped the side of his nose significantly. 'I had a lead which brought me down here, Inspector.'

'And what was that?'

'A tip-off to keep an eye on Nicholas Warren. I couldn't

believe my luck when I found out he ran a guesthouse.'

'It would have been a courtesy to have contacted us.'

'Given time I would have, when I'd something concrete to go on. And I was getting there.'

'What was the tip-off?'

'Only that he'd been seen in the vicinity of a couple of houses that were later robbed. All very vague, but my clients were desperate enough to follow up anything. They're only a small company, and this is stretching them to breaking point.'

He paused. 'Then Helen Campbell arrives out of the blue and announces to all and sundry that her husband's a loss adjuster. I could cheerfully have strangled her. All my softly-softly work gone for a burton. They were going to be very much on their guard after *that* piece of information.'

'You hadn't come across him – Mr Campbell?'

'No, though I've done some work for his firm in the past. I'm told he was up here at the weekend.'

He looked shrewdly at Ledbetter. 'I know Helen came here on Monday; my office is just along the road and I saw her. What did she have to say?'

'You know I can't tell you that, Mr Pike. Sufficient to say that she gave us some very valuable information which might be crucial.'

'Bloody amateurs! There I am, sweating my guts out month after month, and she waltzes in and hands you the solution on a plate! There ain't no justice.'

Ledbetter smiled. 'The country's police forces might agree with you. We haven't been exactly idle ourselves.'

'And is it really all over bar the shouting?'

'Not quite. We still need one vital piece of information, but we hope to have it by the end of the week.'

'Well, you're obviously not going to tell me any more, so all I can do is wish you luck. Meanwhile, presumably, I keep on acting my part of innocent bystander at the Seven Stars.'

'That would be best, sir.'

As Ledbetter watched Pike leave the room, he reflected that Helen Campbell had again been proved correct: Pike's 'innocent bystander' rôle had not deceived her. One very astute lady, Mrs Campbell. Pity they couldn't recruit her into the police force.

There was a phone-call for Helen at lunch-time and she hurried to take it. She'd half-thought it might be Pen, but it was Michael's voice that said in her ear, 'Helen? Is that you?'

'Michael! Oh, thank goodness!'

'Well, that's a better greeting than I expected.'

'I wanted to explain, about leaving the Seven Stars so suddenly.'

'That it wasn't to escape my evil clutches? With all due modesty, I didn't really think so. But I was concerned about you. Why *did* you go and where did you go to?'

She hesitated. 'As to where, I'm at a somewhat down-market B & B in Steeple Bayliss.'

'And as to why?'

'That would take longer to answer.'

'Such as over dinner?'

'That sounds a good idea.'

'I agree; it wasn't the same without you, last night.'

'Have the police asked to see you?'

'Yes, I'm due there at three o'clock. What's it all about, do you know?'

'I'd better leave the inspector to tell you.'

'All right, be mysterious. Shall I call for you at seven-thirty?'

'That would be fine. They eat at six at the new place, so I'll phone and say I won't need a meal.'

'And I must let Kate know. What's your address?'

She gave it to him, and put down the receiver. So after all she would be seeing Michael again, and despite her luke-warm reply to Penelope, her spirits lifted at the prospect.

The phone-call came promptly at eight, and the policemen in the van outside tensed as Nicholas answered it.

The whispering voice on the line sounded oddly sinister. 'Murder was not on the agenda, Warren.'

A hesitation, then Warren's voice: 'I agree it was most

unfortunate. Not intentional, of course – just an instinctive reaction.'

There was a long silence, and the police exchanged anxious glances. Warren said: 'Are you there, sir?'

'Of course I'm here. It must never happen again. No violence of any kind, that was the agreement.'

'I know. I assure you –'

'Tomorrow morning, then, at Ashmartin.' And the phone went dead. A moment later a click indicated that Warren had replaced the receiver.

'Bloody hell!' ejaculated one of the constables. 'The other side of the ruddy county!'

Minutes later, Ledbetter received the information that the call had come from a public call-box in an Ashmartin hotel. There was virtually no chance of identifying the caller.

Ashmartin was the eastern-most town in Broadshire, some fifty miles from Steeple Bayliss. The quickest route was along the M4, and it was arranged that the first in a succession of cars would follow Cain when he left the Seven Stars with the package.

Various plain-clothes men and women would then keep watch on the sorting office, with an unmarked police car standing by round the corner to convey the suspect back to Steeple Bayliss.

The first part of the proceedings went according to plan. Cain delivered the package and drove home, unaccompanied, to the Seven Stars. The police settled down to wait. The morning passed, and then the afternoon. Ledbetter, in constant touch with the police car, was getting restive.

'No sign yet, Happy?'

'Not a glimmer, Guv.'

'There's no way he could have been and gone without your noticing?'

'Not a cat in hell's chance. The place is under a microscope.'

Ledbetter sighed. 'I suppose we'll just have to be patient, then.'

At six o'clock Happy Hopkins phoned in.

'Bad news, Guv. They're closing for the day and there's still been no sign.'

Ledbetter groaned. 'But he's in the town, dammit. What's he waiting for?'

'Perhaps he's in no hurry,' came Happy's lugubrious voice. 'For all we know, he might always wait a day or two before collecting them – a week, even.'

'Thanks a bunch, Happy. That makes me feel much better.' So they'd have to go through all this again tomorrow, the hanging about, the waiting.

He rang Webb to report the lack of progress.

'Chummie couldn't have detected anything on the line, could he? Taken fright?'

'No chance. As Happy says, he might never collect them immediately. Perhaps he waits till he's sure no one is hanging around watching the place.'

'Well, tomorrow's another day. Let's hope it's a better one.'

But Friday was equally unproductive for the waiting detectives. The sorting office at Ashmartin, had it but known, had never been better guarded, but nobody came for Cain's parcel.

Meanwhile, the art and antiques course at Melbray was drawing to a close. The final day was devoted to the Impressionist and Post-Impressionist schools, which were among Helen's favourites, but again she was finding it hard to concentrate.

She and Michael had eaten together both Wednesday and Thursday evenings, but tonight she'd arranged to have dinner with Penelope. What, she wondered, her eyes on the luminous paintings on the screen, would she say when Pen asked about Michael, as she was sure to do? What, after all, was there to say?

Certainly they knew each other better now, had discussed a wide range of topics including each other's marriages, but they had avoided mentioning the future. He knew that she needed to see Andrew again, gauge how they both felt after the break and the disastrous meeting in Steeple Bayliss.

As for herself, one moment she was anxious to get home

and see Andrew, be with him again, and the next she dreaded it. Added to that, she was unsure of her feelings for Michael, though she suspected they would deepen if she allowed them to.

Impatient with herself, she brought her attention back to the lecture. Whatever she decided, it would not be an easy decision, nor a quick one. Time alone held the answer.

But time was given a nudge that evening. At six o'clock, a knock came at the door and the landlady's voice announced there was someone to see her.

Helen, about to change for dinner, hesitated. She was meeting Penelope at the Barley Mow, and not till seven-thirty.

'Is it my daughter?' she called.

'No, a gentleman. I've put him in the front room.'

Michael? But they'd said their goodbyes the previous evening. 'Tell him I'll be down in a minute.'

Hastily she put on some make-up, brushed her hair, and went downstairs. The front room, which she'd previously only glanced into, was drab and unwelcoming, furnished in beige moquette and with a thirties-style tiled fireplace. In front of which Andrew stood, looking at her.

Taken totally by surprise, she could only stare back.

'I rang Pen for your address,' he said. 'I have to speak to you.'

'But – I'm coming home tomorrow.'

'That's just it – I might not be there.' And, at her widening eyes, he added quickly, 'I might have to go up to Scotland. I wanted to explain – and also about Sunday.'

She said steadily, 'Your "colleague"?'

He flushed. 'So you did see her. I wasn't sure, when you didn't say anything. But there was no reason why you shouldn't have met; it was a stupid reaction on my part.'

Helen was in no mood for let-out clauses. 'Pure instinct, I'd have thought, keeping us apart.'

'Helen, she's a trainee valuer. Her name's Charlotte Marsh and I'm taking her round to show her the ropes.'

'Is she your mistress?'

He looked startled. 'For God's sake, I didn't –'

'Is she, Andrew?'

'It was a business trip. How many more times do I have to tell you? Phone the office, if you don't believe me.'

'But you have slept with her?'

His colour deepened. 'This really is pretty irrelevant, you know. All right, damn it, I might have slept with her a couple of times. But it didn't mean anything.'

'Not to you, perhaps.'

'Nor her. She –'

'I was thinking of myself,' Helen cut in. 'Is she here now?'

'Yes, it's a follow-up to Sunday. But that doesn't mean – Look, it was only a couple of times. Three at most. We're not –'

She made a sudden movement with her hand. 'I don't want to hear any more.'

He looked at her, brows drawn together, assessing her volte-face. 'Then perhaps you can tell me who that chap was with you and Pen?'

'I did tell you – one of the lodgers at the Seven Stars.'

'And nothing more? He was eyeing me up pretty carefully.'

'I haven't slept with him, if that's what you're asking.'

Andrew flinched. 'Helen, I really am sorry, but as you said yourself, we're going through a difficult patch.'

'I didn't realize how difficult.'

He put a hand out and let it fall. 'The last couple of weeks have been pretty bleak, you know. I've missed you.'

She gave a choked laugh, and his face darkened. 'I tell you I have. Damn it, let's keep things in proportion. I'm not having an *affair* with Charlotte, there's no commitment.'

'What were you doing here on Sunday?'

'Something was nicked from the museum last week. They asked me to call when the place was closed, to keep disruption to a minimum.'

'So it was nothing to do with the Stately Homes?'

'For once, no. Incidentally, Pen told me you'd been staying at the Seven Stars in the thick of it and helped to wind up the case. Quite the little sleuth, aren't you?'

She didn't reply, and after a moment he went on: 'Still,

to get back to us, I appreciate that Sunday was enough to throw everything into the melting pot, just when we're supposed to be taking stock.'

'I've certainly been doing that these last few days.'

He took her hand. 'It's made me realize what a bloody fool I've been. I want you back, darling, and I swear I'll try to make it work, if you'll give me half a chance. Will you?'

Despite their linked hands, she felt at a distance from him, apart. 'I don't know, Andrew. I really don't know.'

He released her hand. 'Well, you know how I feel. I love you, and I want our marriage to continue. Will you bear that in mind during your deliberations?'

She nodded.

'If I don't get home tomorrow, I'll give you a ring.' He paused, searching her face. 'You will wait for me, won't you?'

'I'll wait till you get back,' she said. Which, for the moment, was as far as she'd commit herself.

The sorting office closed at twelve-thirty on Saturdays, and there had still been no takers for the parcel. The Nymphenberg shepherdess which had cost Lord Cleverley his life lay unclaimed in its cardboard box, and the frustrated detectives drove home.

'It's hellish bad luck, when we're within inches of closing the case,' Webb said to Hannah that evening, as they sat over dinner in her flat. 'Poor Chris is tearing his hair out, but there's damn-all we can do.'

Hannah poured more coffee. 'Do you think it will ever be claimed?'

'God knows. Each passing day makes it more unlikely, in my opinion. We did wonder if he'd surface again after the murder, but when he phoned, we thought we had it made. Didn't expect a slip-up at this stage of the game.'

'It's a pity this last item is one of the less valuable ones.'

'And we still haven't a clue why he wants them. Even the thieves don't know – they just stole to order.'

'Perhaps he's playing a game with you.'

'Oh, he's doing that, all right,' Webb said grimly.

183

'What'll happen to the rest of them?'

'Hardy will go down for five years, possibly ten, the girl much the same if she can get away with manslaughter. Failing that, life.'

Hannah shuddered. 'And the other lot?'

'The two women aren't being charged. I should think Warren will get five years, Cain possibly less, since he wasn't so involved.'

'I wonder if they think it's worth it. How many have they done altogether?'

'Ten country houses, with a few others probably also down to them. At least we know why everything they took was easily portable; it had to be collected from some post office. So much for our theory of the goods being flown out of the country the same day. There they were all the time, wrapped in brown paper and sitting in bloody pigeon-holes in Dewsbury and Liverpool and Clacton-on-Sea.

'It beggars belief, doesn't it? Ming vases and antique silver, taking their chances alongside a parcel of books or some kid's birthday present. Suppose there'd been a hiccup and little Joey had ended up with a diamond-studded picture of Queen Victoria!'

'Worth more than a train set, I should think, even if some of the stones were missing! But he'd probably have swopped it for –'

'What did you say?' Webb's smile had faded.

'I said he'd probably –'

'About the stones?'

'There were some missing; didn't you know?'

'I knew,' Webb said. 'How did you?'

She stared at him. 'It was in the paper.'

'Oh no. We kept that little detail to ourselves. Hannah, for God's sake – this could be important. Where did you hear about the missing stones?'

She thought for a moment. 'I was with someone – Monica, I think. Yes, that's right – it was at Hatherley Hall, at the party.'

'The Rudge place?'

'Yes, we –' She broke off, her eyes widening at the

expression on his face. 'David, you're not thinking what I think you're thinking?'

'It was Sir Clifford who mentioned them?'

She moistened her lips. 'Yes; we were talking about the miniature, and I said I'd read that the frame was studded with diamonds and would that add to the value?'

'Go on. Tell me exactly what he said.'

'He just said some were missing, that's all. Oh God, David, not Sir Clifford!'

But he was already on his way out of the room, snatching up his mobile phone which he'd left on the hall table.

'Ken? Sorry to drag you away from the bosom of your family, but duty calls. Urgently. I'll pick you up at your gate in ten minutes.'

A uniformed maid answered the door and looked at them inquiringly.

'DCI Webb and Sergeant Jackson, to see Sir Clifford Rudge.'

'Is he expecting you?'

'Probably not.'

'Will you wait in the hall then, while I tell him you're here?'

She walked over to the large double doors on the left of the hall. Quite a place, Webb thought, looking at the curving staircase with the gallery at the top. So this was where Frobisher brought Hannah, when she should have been in Paris with him. Still, since her being here had provided the last piece of the puzzle, he was prepared to forgive him.

Jackson shifted from one foot to the other. 'Taking his time about admitting us, Guv.'

'He's an old man, Ken; not likely to abscond out of the window, if that's what you're thinking. Probably having a glass of brandy. He must know why we're here.'

The door opened at last, the maid beckoned them and they walked across the hall and through the doorway into what was obviously the drawing-room. It was a long, beautiful room in shades of grey and pale blue, warmed with splashes of coral in curtains, rug and cushions.

Sir Clifford was standing in front of the fireplace, his wife, frail and elegant, seated on a sofa to his left. He came quickly forward to shake their hands, which, in the circumstances, Jackson found embarrassing. It was hardly a social call.

'Chief Inspector – and Sergeant, is it? A cold night to be out.'

The man's face and voice were familiar from television programmes. No wonder he whispered over the phone.

'Sir Clifford, I'm here to arrest you on –'

'Yes, yes, my dear chap, I know. We don't need to go through it, surely?'

'Then I must caution you –'

'Very well, Chief Inspector, you've done your duty. Now perhaps we can be civilized about this, and sit down? Could I get you a glass of brandy? No? Coffee, then?'

'I've just had some, thank you. Sir Clifford –'

The old man raised his hands in a gesture of resignation. 'All right, since you won't be diverted, we'll get straight down to business. To be frank, I've been debating whether to come and see you. Things started going wrong with that girl on the course; she was staying at the Seven Stars. Pure fluke, of course, but it gave me quite a turn. I began thinking of her as a kind of nemesis.

'But what really clinched it was Bertie Cleverley's death. I was as responsible for it as if I'd dealt the actual blow, and he was one of my oldest friends.'

'Which didn't stop you robbing him, sir.'

The old man smiled ruefully. 'You're quite right, I've no call to wax sentimental.'

Jackson stirred. 'This house was also broken into, wasn't it, sir?'

'It was indeed, Sergeant. A double bluff, in the shape of my Georgian wine-taster. I was extremely thankful to have it back safely, via Wolverhampton sorting office.'

Lady Ursula spoke for the first time. 'It's no good, Clifford, I can't let you do it.'

'My dear –' He started towards her.

'Chief Inspector,' she went on rapidly, 'it was I who was the instigator, not my husband.'

186

The old man's face crumpled. 'Oh, Ursula,' he said sadly.

'He made all the arrangements, of course, but he loathed every moment of it. It was I who coveted those things, and pestered him till he obtained them for me. And it was my greed that caused Bertie's death, my desire for the little shepherdess. Well, I shall never own it now.'

Sir Clifford cleared his throat. 'It's an illness with her, Chief Inspector – she can't help herself.'

'But it was you, sir, who made the arrangements.'

He sighed. 'Yes, and of course I knew it was wrong, but I could never deny my wife anything.'

'Let me try to explain.' Lady Ursula leant forward, her hands clasped. 'I was born into an old, titled family, Chief Inspector, "Lady Ursula" from birth, but there were times I hated that. My schoolfriends taunted me with it, because by then, you see, we were almost destitute.

'My father was the last male heir – a charming, feckless man whom we all adored. But he gambled and drank away the family inheritance and bit by bit everything had to go. My earliest memories are of my mother weeping as she collected together some pieces of jewellery or a treasured miniature to pay his debts. Possessions came to represent security and I began to steal at an early age, to ensure my survival. It became a compulsion.'

'But your husband's a wealthy man, ma'am –'

'Which should have satisfied me? I know.' She looked round the lovely room, at the rosewood writing table, the original paintings, the rich tapestries. 'But no matter what Clifford said, I couldn't regard any of this as *mine*. I needed something of my own, something *secret*, that no one could take away from me.

'In the early days, he pleaded with me to stop, but dearly as I loved him, I couldn't. As he said, it was an illness by that time. So, rather than let me take risks – and make no mistake, I should have gone on stealing – he insisted on doing it for me.'

She gazed reflectively into the fire, twisting the emerald and diamond ring on her finger. Webb stooped suddenly to

187

take her thin, mottled hand in his, turning it so that the jewels blazed in the firelight.

'You recognize it, of course,' she said sadly. 'I stole it from the cloakroom at Randall Tovey's. I have no shame, you see, my friends are not exempt. I even covet their personal trinkets; souvenirs with happy memories I regard as talismans.'

She paused and Sir Clifford took up the story. 'For many years we kept to one object every eighteen months or so, mainly from jewellers and auction houses. It kept Ursula happy and I told myself that such items were covered by insurance. She locked them away, and every now and then she would take them out and handle them. They gave her the security which my love could not.'

Lady Ursula reached up and took hold of his hand. 'Then, one day,' she continued, 'we heard about Nicholas Warren and his success in retrieving that brooch. You know what I'm referring to?'

Webb nodded.

'It seemed the ideal solution, a master planner and a daring thief to carry out the plan. If we could persuade these people to act for us, Clifford need no longer put himself at risk and a whole world of treasure would open up for us. As, indeed, it did.'

She looked up at Webb. 'No doubt you'd like to see our ill-gotten gains. Let me show you.'

She rose and, crossing the room, tilted one of the large pictures and pressed a button behind it. The wall slid soundlessly back to disclose a space about eight feet square, and Webb and Jackson, close behind her, moved forward and looked inside.

One wall was given over to a selection of paintings – a Renoir, a Matisse, two small Corots. The others were lined with shelves and glass-fronted cabinets containing bronzes, enamels, silver and a prodigal heap of jewellery, among which Webb recognized a ruby and diamond necklace belonging to a European princess, stolen from her bedroom at the Savoy.

His eyes went slowly round, registering one after another

of the objects from their circulated descriptions: vinaigrettes, carriage clocks, plaques, and, given equal prominence, the inexpensive trifles whose taking had so puzzled him but whose possession he now knew was supposed to guarantee happiness.

Jackson touched his arm, and with a nod of his head indicated the Victorian miniature with its missing stones which had been Sir Clifford's downfall.

It was as they stood looking at it that two dull, muffled plops sounded in the room behind them. The detectives spun round and dashed back to the fire. It was, of course, too late. The two old people, hands tightly linked, sat side by side on the sofa, each with a small, neat hole in the chest, from which an ugly stain was spreading. Below Sir Clifford's right hand lay a small gun, the half-open table drawer indicating its hiding place.

Webb knelt to feel for pulses, knowing in advance the uselessness of it, and got back to his feet with a shake of his head.

'God, Guv, we shouldn't have fallen for that.' Jackson's voice was shaking.

Webb didn't reply, and the sergeant glanced at him curiously. Or perhaps, he thought suddenly, the Governor *hadn't* fallen for it? Had he guessed Sir Clifford's intention and taken no steps to thwart it? It was not a question he could ask, but, staring down at the two old faces, he couldn't regret the outcome.

As though reading his mind, Webb sighed and turned away. 'I reckon it's all for the best, Ken,' he said.